TAKEN BY THE ORC GENERAL
MAGIC APOCALYPSE #1
Aurelia Skye

BLURB

Her supercollider reopened a portal between Earth and mythical realms. Now mated to their fierce warlord, can their love bridge two colliding worlds?

When quantum physicist Dr. Rianna Goodwin ignores warnings and opens a black hole with the supercollider, the experiment accidentally tears open a portal between Earth and mythical realms that was sealed off centuries ago by human witches. As Mythic Alphas in search of their Omegas flood through, Rianna catches the eye of Halox, the orcs' Supreme General, who claims her as his mate. Compelled by a mystical bond she doesn't understand, Rianna navigates a dangerous new world as she becomes an Omega and surrenders to an intense attraction she can't deny. With humanity on the brink, she and Halox must bridge the divide between their peoples before a looming supernatural threat consumes them all.

This is a spicy fantasy romance featuring fated mates, enemies to lovers, a possessive Alpha hero, and an independent, intelligent woman, who refuses to be subservient. Since it's part of a planned series, there are some plot lines not resolved, but the main romance between Rianna and Halox ends with a HEA.

CHAPTER ONE—RIANNA

The sun crept over the horizon as Dr. Rianna Goodwin strode briskly across the parking lot of the Dowling Center, her heels clicking against the asphalt. As she approached the front doors, raised voices caught her attention.

A large group of protestors bearing signs reading "Stop the Collider" had gathered, blocking the entrance. They chanted slogans as security guards tried unsuccessfully to herd them back. Her shoulders tightened, lips pressing into a thin line. She had no time for this today.

Aislinn Roming stood at the edge of the crowd, wisps of wavy red hair escaping her braid as she shouted encouragement to the protestors through a bullhorn. Her blue eyes blazed with fervor. Rianna changed course, making a beeline for her opposition's leader.

"Call them off, Aislinn," said Rianna heatedly. "This is your last warning."

She lowered the bullhorn and met her gaze unflinchingly. "I can't do that in good conscience. You have to listen to me, Dr.

Goodwin. The forces you intend to unleash could threaten the very fabric of our universe."

"I don't have to listen to anything." She crossed her arms over her chest. "My research will advance human knowledge, despite your obstruction. Now stand down."

The two women faced off, oblivious to the press of bodies around them. The air between them seemed alive with electric tension, two unyielding forces about to collide.

Sensing violence was imminent, the security guards moved in, forming a wedge between the scientists and protestors. Rianna tore her glare away from Aislinn, letting the guards firmly guide the woman back.

Aislinn called desperately over her shoulder, "You have to stop this madness before it's too late."

Rianna turned away, a wall of stoic determination on her face. She wouldn't be deterred from her life's purpose. Not when she was so close to answers that could reshape human understanding.

Squaring her shoulders, she strode through the newly opened path to the doors, ignoring the protestors' shouted insults. Their ignorance wouldn't sway her rational mind. She swiped her ID badge forcefully, entering the lobby as Aislinn's frantic pleas faded behind her.

Today would change everything. No one could stop it now.

The familiar sterile scent of the lobby washed over her as the doors swung shut, muting the tumult outside. She took a deep breath, steadying her scattered nerves. This was her domain, her temple of science and reason. Here, logic reigned supreme.

At the elevators, her mind raced with thoughts of everything that had led up to this moment—the sleepless nights poring over data, the endless calculations, the setbacks and breakthroughs. It had all come down to this day and this test that would validate her life's work.

The elevator arrived at the control room, the doors

whispering open to reveal a hive of activity. Technicians bustled about, engrossed in final checks and preparations. The buzz of tense excitement filled the air.

Rianna stepped out, the click of her heels sharp against the tile floor. She set down her notes with a thump, straightened her pristine white lab coat, and called out crisply, "Status report."

Her senior technicians responded in rapid succession, voices clipped and focused. Rianna moved briskly about the room, inspecting monitors and settings as they continued their reports. Pressure valves had been primed. Secondary cooling systems were standing by. All diagnostics were green across the board.

Satisfied, she took her place at the central command station overlooking the vast collider chamber below. She allowed herself a deep, steadying breath before keying the microphone. "Commencing supercollider activation in T-minus sixty seconds and counting." Her voice echoed through the building's intercoms.

An electric hush fell over the control room, broken only by the low hum of machinery and her team's controlled breathing. She kept her eyes fixed on the primary monitors as the countdown timer ticked lower, each second feeling weighted and eternal.

This was the culmination of half a decade of sacrifice and tireless work pursuing a dream few dared imagine possible, and now success was so close she could taste it. Her heart thundered against her ribs.

"Three…two…one…" Her thumb nudged the ignition switch forward. "Supercollider activated."

For a long, breathless moment, all was still and silent save for the growing thrum of power building in the giant collider ring below. Monitors remained dark, turbines not yet kicked into full gear.

Then needles jumped on dials as readings surged. A low

vibration shivered through the room. Data spat across screens in hypnotic cascades of numbers and graphs too rapid to track. A distant rumble built until it became a bone-rattling roar.

She held her breath for a second. This was it. The culmination of her life's passion, and her vision tunneled down to a single monitor displaying the supercollider's core.

A tiny, swirling dot of darkness blossomed at the center, steadily growing as particles accelerated to near light-speed. It swelled into a ravenous black hole, consuming all matter and light pulled into its grasp. Warning klaxons wailed, but she paid them no mind. This void was expected, and she was sure it was something they could sustain and control.

She watched, enraptured, as the simulated singularity expanded past theoretical diameters. Still, it grew, as if possessing a will of its own. Her brow creased in consternation as a prickle of unease hit her. That couldn't be right. Her calculations indicated it should have stabilized by now.

Anxiety licked an icy path down her spine. She opened her mouth to shout the emergency shutdown sequence, but before she could form the words, a high-pitched whine pierced the room. It climbed rapidly in intensity until humans could no longer process the audible assault. She clapped her hands over her ears in agony along with her reeling team.

Then, soundlessly, the shrieking void collapsed in upon itself, replaced by something far more terrifying than even her brilliant mind could have conceived. Reality itself tore open before her disbelieving eyes. A shimmering vortex of energy speared through the collider room, blinding and hypnotic. It was beautiful, pearlescent, and rippling with colors no human eyes could fully comprehend. It was utterly, impossibly wrong.

Her great rational mind shuddered to a halt, unable to accept or process what she was seeing. This couldn't be real. It defied every natural law upon which the universe was built.

Yet her team stared just as agape at the phenomenon, many collapsing to their knees or shielding their vision against the crawling radiance. No, this was no hallucination or dream. It was a warped reality.

The vortex stabilized, undulating gently. From its center, dark forms slowly took shape, lumbering forth and passing through the viscous light membrane as if stepping through a semi-solid waterfall.

Her eyes widened in horror and disbelief as the forms shambled closer with thunderous footfalls. Monsters. Beasts from the darkest depths of myth made real flesh before her. Giants with curved rams' horns. Creatures with moldy gray skin, weeping sores, and elongated, crooked limbs, and more beasts for which she had no name.

A cacophony of screams, roars, and unnatural sounds pelted her senses as the tide of monsters continued to spill out from the rippling portal. The abstract theories Rianna had clung to now took monstrous shape before her eyes. She had been so very wrong...

One beast paused, perhaps ten feet away, twitching and scenting the air with flared nostrils. Slowly it turned, fixing glowing lilac eyes that were incongruous with its otherwise rugged appearance upon her. Being pinned by that gaze cut through the haze of chaos and terror.

Those alien eyes pierced Rianna to her core, and she knew with sudden, impossible certainty that it saw her. Truly saw her.

Recognition slammed into Rianna's mind even before the monster rumbled a single guttural word.

"Mate."

The beast, an orc, barreled toward her with thundering steps. Her paralysis broke, and she spun on her heel and ran, the pounding footfalls of the monster giving chase echoing down the hallway behind her.

This was no longer her world of logic and reason. This was a realm of nightmares made real, and she had brought it into being.

Her heart beat erratically, her mind a whirl of terror and disbelief. The orc, a tall, broad, and muscular creature with green skin and long green-black hair in braids, followed her. Its lilac eyes had looked into her soul, recognizing something she couldn't fathom, and it had called her "Mate."

What did that mean? How could that be?

Behind her, the orc's heavy footsteps thundered like a monstrous drumbeat. It was gaining, each footfall an ominous echo of her mounting fear. She dared not look back, focusing only on the twisting corridors ahead.

It wasn't just the orc's sheer physical presence that terrified her. There was intelligence in those eyes. A purpose. The thing knew what it wanted, and it had chosen her.

"MATE," it bellowed again, its voice a bone-chilling growl that resonated through Rianna's very being.

She reached a crossroads of hallways and skidded to a halt, panic clawing at her throat. Which way? Any choice could mean life or death.

There was no time to decide. The orc was too close. Its deep, grunting breaths filled the air with a musky, wild scent like damp earth and primal aggression.

Her body moved on instinct, propelling her down the right-hand passage. Her vision swam, everything a blur except the overpowering need to escape, to flee from the embodiment of raw, untamed power hot on her heels.

Her mind raced, searching for any understanding of the creature pursuing her. Orcs were fictional creatures of fantasy and legend. They weren't real. They couldn't be real.

Yet this one was. Its presence was undeniable, its form unlike anything she had ever seen. Its towering frame was corded with muscle, its face a chiseled blend of brute force and strange, inhuman beauty. The braids of its green-black hair swayed with movement, its lilac eyes glowing with a hunger Rianna couldn't comprehend. Was it male? She felt somehow certain he was.

The absurdity of her thoughts struck her. She was analyzing the creature as if he were a scientific specimen, even as he hunted her with relentless determination. That was a reflection of her life's obsession with understanding, a drive that had brought her to this nightmarish reality.

The corridor ahead ended abruptly in a dead end that trapped her. Rianna's breath caught in her throat. No, it couldn't end like this. There had to be a way out.

She frantically searched for an escape, her eyes landing on a ventilation shaft high on the wall. Without a second thought, she grabbed a nearby cart, scrambling atop it. She reached for the shaft, fingers grasping at the cold metal.

The orc's roar filled the corridor, a sound of frustration and anger. He had seen her, understood her intent, and was almost upon her.

CHAPTER TWO—RIANNA

Her fingers closed around the cold metal of the vent. It was her only chance, and she didn't waste a moment. Hoisting herself up, she scrambled inside just as the orc reached the cart, his roar a terrible symphony of rage and thwarted desire. The musky scent was overpowering, making her head swim as she pulled herself into the shaft, legs kicking wildly as she sought purchase. She heard the orc's thunderous arrival, his furious snarl echoing through the confined space.

Her legs found traction, and she began to crawl, the narrow passage pressing in on her from all sides. The sound of metal wrenching reached her ears as the orc tore at the shaft, his immense strength seeking to breach her last refuge.

His growls grew distant as she crawled farther into the labyrinthine ductwork, but she was certain the creature wouldn't stop. He would hunt her relentlessly, driven by an urge she didn't understand.

The fear began to ebb, replaced by a cold determination.

Rianna Goodwin was no helpless prey. She was a scientist and a seeker of truth. She had unleashed this nightmare, and she would find a way to contain it.

But first, she had to survive.

As she continued her crawling escape, her mind began to work, analyzing and strategizing. The orc had recognized her and had spoken a human word. There was intelligence there, a connection to be explored, so maybe she could…reason with it?

What did he want from her? Why had he singled her out?

The answers were elusive, but the questions were a lifeline, a way to navigate the chaos she had unleashed and keep herself composed. She clung to them, letting them guide her through the darkness toward an uncertain future where logic and reason had been replaced by the raw, primal forces of a world gone mad.

Somewhere in that madness lurked the orc, his lilac eyes filled with an inscrutable longing, his massive form a mystery she must unravel.

The beast had called her his mate, which was a word laden with meaning and intent. Maybe it held the key to understanding the terror she had awakened. The word echoed in her mind, a haunting refrain that wouldn't let her go. A word that, despite everything, sent a strange thrill through her, a fascination she couldn't deny.

She shook her head, banishing the thought. Now wasn't the time for such distractions. She had work to do. Her breath came in short rasps when she finally emerged from the vent, dropping into an alley. Her legs were weak, and her body trembled from the relentless chase. She had to keep moving, to find Aislinn and figure out what was happening.

The city was alive around her, a maze of lights and sounds that she navigated on autopilot. Her mind was elsewhere, replaying the day's events and searching for answers in the chaos of her thoughts.

The sound of her own breathing was loud in Rianna's ears as she stumbled through the city's twisting corridors. Fear and disbelief gnawed at her, the orc's thundering footfalls echoing in her mind as she continuously looked behind her, searching for any sign of his continued pursuit.

"Mate." He roared it from behind her, sounding somewhat distant but not leaving her optimistic about her chances of escape.

His bellowing cry resonated in her soul, leaving her chilled and shaking. How had this happened? Orcs were supposed to be fictional creatures of fantasy and legend, not chasing her through the city streets.

Her body reacted to his presence in ways she couldn't understand. The musky, wild scent of him stirred something deep within her, a primal attraction she couldn't shake, but fear was the driving force now, propelling her forward as she sought escape. The orc's pursuit was relentless, each step bringing him closer. She could almost feel his hot breath on her neck and hear the grunt of his breath as he gained ground.

Skidding around a corner, her heart leaped into her throat as she found herself trapped in another dead end. Panic surged, her mind racing as she frantically searched for a way out.

The orc's roar filled the air, a sound of irritation and fury that made her blood run cold. He was almost upon her, his towering frame a terrifying blend of brute strength and brutal beauty.

Hearing his footsteps made her take a deep breath and turn to face him as he stood at the entryway of the alley. She was face to face with him. His lilac eyes were ablaze, his breath audible as he advanced.

"Who are you?" She gasped, stumbling back. "What do you want with me?"

"You're mine." His answer was virtually a snarl, his voice a raw, primal force.

Her body betrayed her, reacting to his pheromones in a way

she couldn't comprehend. Desire and terror warred within her, leaving her paralyzed.

With a sound almost like a purr, the orc grabbed her, pressing her against the wall, his face inches from hers. His breath was hot, a primitive scent that sent shivers down her spine. There was intent in his lilac eyes, a wild hunger she couldn't quite comprehend.

His head lowered to her neck, and she felt his nostrils flare as he inhaled deeply, taking in her scent. A strange noise escaped him, something between a growl and a purr, vibrating against her skin as he rubbed his nose along her jawline.

"What are you doing?" She meant to demand an answer, but her voice was reedy. Her heart pounded, and a confusing mix of terror and something else twisted in her gut. Her panties were abruptly damp, which made him inhale more forcefully. She was trapped, held by a frightening and intoxicating force.

"You," He rumbled, his voice deep and guttural, "Are mine."

His breath against her skin was warm and damp as he continued to inhale her scent while rubbing his face against hers. His lips brushed against her neck, a fleeting touch that left her reeling.

"I'm not yours." She finally remembered to struggle against his iron grip. "Let me go."

His only response was a deeper inhalation, his mouth now open against her skin, tasting her, and…marking her with his scent. She didn't understand how she knew, but she sensed it was something like that.

A bolt of sensation shot through her, a reaction she couldn't control or understand. Her body was betraying her, responding to his touch in a way that defied logic.

"You don't understand yet." His voice was a rough growl that vibrated against her. "You will."

With a surge of adrenaline, she found the strength to fight

back. "I understand enough," she snapped, her knee connecting with his groin.

He roared in pain, his hold on her loosening for just a second, but it was enough. She slipped free, her mind a whirl of confusion and fear.

"You won't get away from me," he said, his voice tinged with pain and determination.

"I'll take my chances." She turned to run, but his words lingered, a haunting promise that filled her with doubt. She was oddly sure the mark he'd left was more than physical. It was a claim, a bond she couldn't quite comprehend, but she knew about it on an instinctive level.

As she fled through the city's twisting corridors, one thought rang clear. The orc had marked her as his own, and he would stop at nothing to make her his. Her escape was only the beginning, and the chase was far from over.

Her lungs burned and her feet ached from the relentless chase. She had managed to escape for now, but the terror still gnawed at her. An orc. A real, living orc had held her, his hot breath on her neck a lingering reminder of its pursuit.

Her mind reeled. Orcs weren't real, but she had felt it. He was as real as the fear that consumed her—and Aislinn Roming had warned her. Rianna had dismissed her as a superstitious fool and ridiculed her beliefs in magic and barriers, but now, with the reality of the orc's pursuit still fresh in her mind, she couldn't deny the truth.

Aislinn had been right.

She made her way through the darkened streets, her thoughts a whirl of confusion and fear. She needed answers, and there was only one person who could provide them. Aislinn.

Since Aislinn and her group had been persistent, Mr. Dowling had run a thorough background check on her. Rianna had seen the report, and with her eidetic memory, she'd naturally memorized the woman's address. Now, she headed in that direction, wondering if the opposition leader would help her. After all, she'd been clear about the dangers, and Rianna had ignored her. How could she face her now?

What choice was there besides waiting for the orc to catch her and surrendering to him? The thought filled her with excitement that she ruthlessly squashed.

After running through the myriad dramas unfolding on the streets around her, evading anyone who reached for or noticed her, she finally arrived at the other woman's door, her hand hesitating before she knocked. She hadn't even touched the wood when the door creaked open, and Aislinn's eyes met hers in a knowing, almost accusatory gaze.

"You were right," Rianna blurted out, the words catching in her throat. "About the portal and the danger. An orc…lots of creatures…came through. The orc chased me and marked me. I don't understand any of it, but I need your help."

Her eyes narrowed as her lips pressed into a thin line. "I warned you," she said, her voice cold. "I told you what would happen, and you didn't listen."

"I know." Tears welled in her eyes. "I know, and I'm sorry, but please, I need your help. I need to understand what's happening and how to stop it."

A long silence filled the room, the weight of Aislinn's judgment heavy in the air. Finally, she stepped aside, her voice softening. "Come in. We'll talk."

She struggled to catch her breath from all the exertion as she stepped into the room, a mixture of relief and trepidation washing over her. She had come to her former adversary for help, and now, they were in this together.

They had to be.

The barrier had been breached, and the world as they knew it had changed forever. Rianna's mistake had brought them here, and now, they would face the consequences. The orc's mark was still fresh on her neck, a symbol of a reality she could no longer deny. The battle had just begun.

CHAPTER THREE—RIANNA

An unnatural calm filled the room, as if time itself had come to a halt. Aislinn's apartment was like a secret sanctuary, a place untouched by the chaos of New York City. Ancient books lined the shelves, and the scent of herbs and old parchment lingered in the air.

Rianna's eyes darted to the hidden corners, a sense of foreboding settling in her stomach. Her neck still burned from the mark, a constant reminder of the orc, and what she had done. "Tell me what happened."

"You opened the portal." She motioned for Rianna to sit down. "Do you have any idea what that means?"

Rianna's hands trembled as she took a seat, the weight of her stare heavy upon her. "I didn't know. I didn't understand." She looked down at her hands. "I never bothered to read the literature you sent me after the first paragraph mentioned the old ways and magic."

For a second, she looked angry, but then her face softened,

the hardness in her eyes giving way to something more compassionate. "I figured you didn't, and I doubt you meant this to happen, but remorse doesn't change what has occurred."

She blinked back tears as the reality of her situation began to sink in. She had unleashed something terrifying and beyond her comprehension.

"Millennia ago, the Earth was a nexus point for the other realms. Human women were especially desired because Alphas could trigger us to be Omegas."

Rianna didn't understand her words, or at least the context. "What?"

She sighed. "The barrier was put in place for a reason. It was meant to protect us, to keep the dangers of the other realms at bay, and now, because of your actions, it's breached."

The words stung, a harsh truth she couldn't deny. She had acted without thinking, driven by curiosity and defiance, and now the world had changed. "What do we do?" she asked, her voice breaking. "How do we fix it?"

Aislinn's eyes met hers, steely resolve in her gaze. "We can't undo what's been done," she said, her voice firm. "The barrier has been breached, and only magic can close it. Maybe. There might not be enough magic or enough users left to reseal the portal or strengthen the barrier." She looked fretful for a moment. "Magic will return to those who have the talent for it, so maybe there's hope, but it won't be an immediate option."

Her head hurt thinking about all these things. As a woman of science, it made no sense, but she couldn't pretend it wasn't happening. "You say the portal was closed for a reason? Why?"

The other woman's blue eyes darkened, a storm of emotions passing through them as she leaned back in her chair. The room seemed to grow still as if the very air was holding its breath, waiting for her to speak.

"The reason the portal was closed goes back to a time when magic was as common as the air we breathe. A time when magical creatures roamed freely, and Earth was a place of wonder and danger in equal measure."

She paused, her gaze far away, lost in memories Rianna couldn't begin to fathom. "The creatures that came through the portal were unlike anything the world had ever seen. They were powerful, beautiful, and terrifying. They were Alphas, driven by a primal need to mate and claim."

Her hands clenched into fists, a tremor of anger passing through her. "And claim they did. Mostly women were marked as Omegas, their very biology changed and twisted to suit the desires of these creatures. The Alphas were relentless, some taking without consent, driven by their biological imperative without attempting to temper their actions."

A gasp escaped Rianna's lips, the horror of it settling deeply in her bones. Her mind raced, images of the orc that had marked her flashing before her eyes. A connection she couldn't deny, a pull that defied logic and reason, and a murky sense of memory, as though she knew all about this on an instinctive level.

Aislinn's voice softened, her anger giving way to a deep sadness. "Not all were cruel. Some sought true connection and true love. They believed in consent, in a bond that went beyond mere biology."

"We were ideal mates, but most Alphas sought to control us. Human men were mostly expendable unless an Alpha Mythic chose to breed with him. Our foremothers got tired of being virtually enslaved." She reached out, her hand finding Rianna's, the touch a comforting anchor. "The witches and magic wielders saw the destruction, the pain, and the chaos. They knew something had to be done, so they joined together, combining all magic in our world to create a spell that would cast out the creatures and close the portal."

Her eyes glistened with unshed tears, the weight of

centuries of memories bearing down on her. "The spell was so powerful that it bound all the magic in the world, using it to feed the spell that kept the portal closed. The magical creatures were ejected, and our world was fully human once more."

Her heart ached, the tragedy of it all a heavy burden. "And now," she whispered, her voice trembling, "I've undone it all."

Aislinn's face tightened, a mask of controlled emotion settling over her features as she withdrew her hand. Her eyes, once filled with compassion, now held a glimmer of reproach. The room suddenly felt cold, the walls closing in on Rianna.

"I tried to warn you, Rianna," said Aislinn, her voice laced with a bitterness she couldn't quite conceal. "For weeks, I begged you to stop, to consider the consequences of your experiments, but you wouldn't listen."

"I didn't believe you," Rianna whispered, tears streaming down her face. "I thought it was all just stories and myths, and your group was crazy. I never thought it could be real."

Aislinn turned away, her body rigid, her posture a clear indication of her disappointment. She moved to the window, staring out at the world that had been forever changed, her silence a heavy weight that filled the room. "My group isn't crazy. We're the last magic users remaining, and our task is to guard the portal. I'm the Keeper." She didn't explain what that was as she fell into a brooding silence.

Her mind raced, the enormity of her mistake settling over her like a dark cloud. She had acted out of arrogance and a need to prove herself, to challenge the boundaries of science, and in doing so, she had ripped open a portal to a world filled with danger and darkness. "I'm so sorry," she choked out, her voice breaking with emotion. "I never meant for any of this to happen. Please tell me there's a way to fix it."

Her shoulders slumped, the anger seeming to drain from her as she turned to face Rianna. Her eyes were filled with a sadness that spoke of loss and regret. "I'm the Keeper of the memories and the records, so I know the spell they used inside and out. There's no way to undo what's been done. The creatures are returning. We can't close the portal, not without a lot more magic, and even then, it might be impossible."

She crossed the room, her steps slow and deliberate as she stopped to stand before her. She reached forward, and for a second, Rianna thought she might slap her. Instead, the other woman pushed back her long fall of curly dark hair, eyeing her neck.

"Oh, no." Aislinn closed her eyes and breathed deeply. Her expression was hard to read when she opened them again. "Tell me what this is? How did you get it?"

Rianna's hand instinctively went to her neck, fingers brushing over the mark that still throbbed, a constant reminder of the orc and the world she had inadvertently exposed. Her breath caught in her throat, heart pounding as she met Aislinn's searching gaze.

"It's a mark," she stammered, the words heavy with a significance she couldn't fully grasp. "An orc gave it to me by rubbing his face against mine. He said I was his, though I rejected that idea. I told you about it when I first arrived."

"I guess I missed that part," she said in a weak voice as her face paled, her eyes widening with shock and concern. She took a step back, her body trembling. "Marked." Her voice was barely above a whisper, the word laced with fear and disbelief. "Do you know what that means? Do you understand what's happening?"

Rianna shook her head, tears welling. "I don't. I didn't ask for this and don't want it."

Her hand came up to cover her mouth, her expression alternating between anger, sorrow, and pity. She turned away, her shoulders shaking as she fought to compose herself.

"This changes everything," she said, her voice thick with emotion. "The mark means he claimed you as his mate. It's a connection…a link between you and the orc. A bond that can't be broken."

Her eyes met Rianna's again when she turned around once more, the depth of her sorrow evident in her gaze. "You've been marked as an Omega, Rianna. You've been claimed by an Alpha. Your very biology has begun to change, twisted to suit his desires."

Her knees gave way, and she stumbled, collapsing into a chair as the room spun around her. The words echoed in her mind, a terrible truth she couldn't escape. She was an Omega, claimed by an Alpha, forever bound to a creature she didn't even know. "What does that mean?" she whispered, her voice hollow with despair. "What does it mean for me? For my life?"

"He'll find you." Aislinn's statement hung in the air, a foreboding pronouncement that sent an icy dart down Rianna's spine. Heavy silence followed, filled with the unspoken implications of what she'd said. "He'll find you," she said again, her voice low and full of dread. "That's what the claim means. You're his now, and he'll stop at nothing to have you."

The words struck her like a physical blow. She looked up at Aislinn with terror, her breath coming in ragged gasps. "How? How can he find me?" she asked, her voice quivering with fear. "What can we do to stop him?"

Her expression was drawn, the lines of worry etched deep in her features. She moved closer, her hand reaching out to grasp Rianna's, squeezing it tightly as if to lend her strength. "The bond between an Alpha and an Omega is powerful, ancient, and magically formed. It transcends distance and time. He'll be drawn to you, guided by instincts and urges he might not even understand."

Her body went limp as the implications sunk in. Nausea hit her as the room spun around her. An Omega? The very word sent shivers down her spine. She couldn't be an Omega, couldn't be claimed by some strange, unknown creature. She didn't even fully understand what an Omega was, so how could she be one just like that?

"I can't be an Omega," she said, her voice filled with panic and disbelief. "I can't be. There must be some mistake. There has to be a way to undo this. Tell me there's a way."

Aislinn's eyes were filled with sympathy and understanding, but also a hint of resignation. "We can try a cleansing ritual," she said softly, her voice gentle. "It's a powerful spell that can purify and remove magical marks, but I must warn you, the bond between Alpha and Omega is strong. I've never heard of it being broken except by the death of one partner."

"I don't care." Rianna cried and scrubbed at her cheeks, desperation clawing at her throat. "We have to try. We have to do something. I can't be his. I won't be." The idea of mating with the orc filled her with horror even as a small part of her seemed like it sprang to life after being dormant for far too long. "No."

Aislinn nodded, her face set with determination. "We'll try, but you have to be prepared for the possibility that it might not work."

"I understand. I'll do whatever it takes."

Without another word, she led Rianna to a small chamber filled with candles, herbs, and mystical symbols. "This is my spell room." She began to chant, her voice a melodious song that filled the air with power and magic. Rianna felt a tingling sensation and warmth that spread through her body, centering on the mark on her neck.

The room glowed with an eerie light, the air thick with the scent of sage and lavender. Time seemed to stretch and warp, the ritual consuming them and drawing her into a world of magic and mysticism. She would have dismissed it all as bunk just hours before, but now she believed with wholehearted desperation.

As the minutes ticked past, it became clear the spell wasn't working. The mark remained, stubborn and unyielding as it resisted all Aislinn's magic. Despite their efforts, the bond was too strong and too deeply ingrained to be severed.

"It's not effective," said Aislinn, her voice weary as the tingling sensation stopped, and the eerie glow faded. "I'm sorry. The bond is too strong, and I can't break it."

Her heart sank, a cold dread settling in her stomach. She was trapped by a destiny she didn't want and a fate she couldn't escape. "What do we do now?" she whispered, tears of frustration and fear threatening to fall again.

"We prepare. We learn what we can, we train others whose magic awakens, and you get ready to face him." Her mouth firmed in a hard line. "They won't find us so easily enslaved this time. If they won't accept partnerships, it's up to us to fight with everything we have…even if we have to fight our new natures to do that."

A sudden chill filled the room, a dark foreboding that sent a shiver down Rianna's spine.

"He's tracked you here and is coming for you."

The Alpha was coming, drawn by the unbreakable bond, guided by a primal need to claim what was his, and she could sense his approach.

They were running out of time.

CHAPTER FOUR—RIANNA

Tension filled the air as her gaze followed the Keeper. Aislinn reached into a hidden compartment and pulled out a thick, leather-bound book. Ancient symbols adorned its cover, and Rianna felt a strange pull toward it. "What's this?"

"A grimoire. It's a book of spells, and you must learn them" Her expression was grave. "Relearning the magic and spreading the knowledge could be our only chance. Memorize them and pass them on."

"Me?" Rianna's voice wavered, her eyes widening in disbelief. "You think I can use magic?"

Aislinn's eyes softened, her fingers brushing the book's cover. "The magic is there, waiting to be accessed by those with latent talents or powers. Since your Alpha found you so quickly, and he's marked you, that should allow you to practice magic. Being an Omega makes it easier to connect to the powers around you. You have to at least try."

A sudden noise cut through the room, a distant rumble that

made her freeze and moan, mostly in fear and partly in longing. The room seemed to tremble, and a feeling of dread settled over her. "He's here."

Aislinn nodded, looking solemn.

Her breath came in ragged gasps. She felt a connection she couldn't explain and a presence she couldn't ignore. The door burst open, and a massive figure filled the doorway, his eyes piercing lilac, his body powerful and imposing. "You." Her lips felt numb as she said the word.

"I am Halox." His deep voice was slightly like rocks grinding together, but there was heat there too. He fixed her with a hungry gaze that made her skin feel itchy and unbearably tight. "You bear my mark. You're mine."

Aislinn stepped forward, her body tense. "Rianna's not yours. She doesn't belong to you."

Halox's eyes narrowed, his lips curling into a sneer. "She bears my mark. She's my mate."

The word 'mate' echoed in Rianna's mind, a terrible truth she couldn't escape. She took a step toward him, lulled into a state she couldn't explain, and prepared to surrender.

Aislinn's hand shot out, a blinding flash of light filling the room. "This is just a distraction spell. It won't last long, so run."

She froze for another second, staring at her mate. No, the orc. The impossible monster before her.

"Run, Rianna." Aislinn's shout broke through her shock, and she stumbled toward the door, her legs carrying her away from the room and away from Halox. Each step felt painful, but on a soul-deep level rather than physically.

She ran through winding hallways of the brownstone, the grimoire clutched tightly in her hands. She found a small alcove, her body trembling as she hid and listened for sounds of his approach.

Time seemed to stretch, each moment an eternity as she waited, body tense while she held her breath. When she didn't hear his heavy footfalls, she allowed herself to breathe, her mind turning to the grimoire. She had to escape the building before he found her so she could study it.

Feeling grimly like it wouldn't matter anyway, she left the brownstone and cut through several alleyways before being unable to go farther, at least for a few minutes. She slipped into a shopping center, losing herself in a quiet corner. The place was deserted, which was unusual for a busy afternoon in New York City.

She curled into a ball on a bench near a fountain, needing to rest. The grimoire was heavy in her hands, and she squinted in the afternoon light pouring in through the windows as she opened it. The very first spell was surprisingly in English, and she whispered it aloud. As soon as she did, the entire book became more than a jumble of symbols and words she didn't recognize. She doubted the original page was in English either. It had been a key to unlock the rest, and she suspected it would only work for someone who had magic.

She scanned the pages, absorbing the ancient spells and incantations. Her eidetic memory made memorization easy, the words and symbols imprinting themselves in her mind, though comprehending them was much harder.

Before she had a chance to test any, she heard a noise deeper in the mall. Gathering her tattered strength, she rushed out of the building, running blindly until she reached Central Park. Hoping to find some cover there, she plunged into the trees, her mind clouded by exhaustion. The trees were a blur, each step a fight against the overwhelming urge to collapse. Every sound was a threat, and every shadow a potential trap.

Ahead, a glimmer of moonlight appeared through the canopy, guiding her forward. How could it be nighttime already? Had she lost track of time, or had the portal opening altered the passage of time itself when it rewrote their reality?

As she broke through the treeline, she froze. A figure stood in the clearing, his back to her, his lilac eyes hidden. Halox.

Panic surged, but her feet were rooted to the spot, her body betraying her. She wanted to flee, yet something pulled her closer.

Her hands trembled as she clutched the ancient leather-bound book, mind conjuring some of the angular runes and arcane symbols etched upon its pages. She immediately turned to a spell to obscure one's scent. Her memory hadn't led her wrong, and she whispered it.

She couldn't be sure it actually worked, but after a moment, he turned and rushed away. Maybe it hadn't even been Halox. It could have been another orc hunting his Omega. He wouldn't stop until he'd tracked her.

That thought brought another unwelcome one. Halox would find her. It was only a matter of time. The mystical claim mark he'd placed on her neck ensured it, and she doubted a scent-masking spell would fool him for long.

Thinking about that moment in his arms, she could still feel the heat of his breath on her neck and the brush of his lips as he'd inhaled her scent and rumbled that single guttural word—"Mine." Her fingers reached up instinctively, hovering over the invisible tether binding her to the monstrously powerful orc warrior.

With an effort, she staggered back into the trees, finding what she hoped was a protected vantage point surrounded by limbs and lush foliage, since it was summer, and the trees hadn't started shedding their leaves yet. She crawled into the makeshift den as deeply as she could, trying not to think about the insects that shared the space with her. Understanding their place in the ecosystem didn't make them any less creepy-crawly to her.

Her eyes threatened to close, but she blinked and jerked up her head as she wrenched her thoughts back to the book in her hands. The sorcerous knowledge therein was now her only hope of surviving Halox's inevitable arrival.

She'd made a lot of progress toward memorizing them at

the mall but employing that knowledge would be another matter entirely. Unlike Aislinn, she didn't know if she possessed any real talent for spellcasting, and modern humans had lost much of the magic wielded in eras past.

Still, she had to try. The life she'd always known depended on it.

Hours passed in a blur of study, the words obscuring on the page before her exhausted eyes. She had reached the limits of what her memory could absorb for now. The rest would have to come through practice.

The next night, after resting fitfully and continuing to move while almost continuously uttering the scent-masking spell, she surveyed the abandoned building where she'd taken shelter. It had once been an asylum but hadn't been opened for years. If she'd cast it properly, a warding spell masked her presence for now, but the Alpha could track her here eventually. She had to keep moving. Staying anywhere for too long was dangerous.

Phone in hand, using it as a flashlight since it wasn't useful for anything else with all the networks down, she navigated the dilapidated hallways of the old hospital, senses straining for any sign of pursuit. It beat almost on constant refrain in her mind. He was coming, and she had to evade him. She tried to ignore the strange sensation that part of her longed to do the opposite—to stop running and let him find her.

Turning a corner, she froze. An imposing silhouette stood outlined at the end of the corridor. Fear lanced through her, and she reacted on instinct, chanting the words to activate a concealment charm. A sense she didn't recognize but couldn't ignore told her it was Halox.

The figure paused, head cocked as if sniffing prey just out of reach. Then he turned and strode away. Rianna sagged back against the wall, breathing raggedly. A close call, but the magic had worked. Barely. Her safety was only an illusion, one that could shatter at any moment. The second she lost focus on the spell, she'd lose its protection.

She quickened her pace, taking a winding route down decaying stairwells to the building's basement. If she could make it to the storm drains, they might provide an escape from this place.

Kneeling by the grimy wall, she carefully pried away the metal grate covering a drain access. The opening yawned darkly before her, the faint trickle of water audible in its depths. Grimacing in distaste, she slipped her legs into the hole, shimmying down into the unknown.

The descent was precarious, her shoes slipping on damp stone, but she soon reached the passage below. Stooped low, she sloshed forward into the shadows. The fetid smell wrinkled her nose, but she stifled the urge to gag. Better this stench than the musky primal scent of the orc who hunted her.

Liar, whispered a voice in her head, reminding her how tantalizing that scent was.

Time lost meaning in the claustrophobic darkness. She wasn't sure how long she'd been navigating the tunnels when she reached a junction point. She paused, wavering. Each direction looked equally uninviting. Her eidetic memory was no help in this labyrinth.

Squaring her shoulders, she chose a path at random, trusting her instincts. The water deepened as she went, soaking the hem of her tattered lab coat. She shivered, from fear or chill she wasn't sure.

Rounding a bend, she came up short. A massive silhouette filled the passage ahead. The glowing animal shine of a lilac gaze cut through the shadows, locking onto her. A familiar musky scent filled her nostrils even as a guttural voice rumbled, "Mine."

Halox had found her.

Panic surged through Rianna. She backpedaled, mind racing

through defensive spells. The orc barreled forward, massive arms grasping for her.

At the last second, she managed to suck in a breath and scream out the words to a disorientation charm. He stumbled, dazedly shaking his head. Rianna didn't hesitate, plunging into the frigid water and scrambling down a side passage.

His enraged roar echoed behind her as she hauled herself up a rusty ladder to the surface. She had escaped, but her lungs burned from exertion and fear. How much longer could this desperate game of pursuit and evasion continue?

Over the next week, Rianna moved constantly between abandoned buildings, storm drains, and even the subway tunnels, but Halox tracked her relentlessly, their near misses draining her mentally and physically.

In her feverish study of the grimoire spells, she meticulously committed each to memory, but putting them into practice remained a challenge. Her spellcasting faltered when under threat, the magic as slippery as water between her desperate fingers.

Late one night, as she picked her way across an old subway platform, she sensed the now familiar tingle of Halox's presence. Too late, she whirled, only to collide with his broad chest.

Strong arms enveloped her in an iron grip. His eyes smoldered like starlit amethysts inches from her own. Warm breath caressed her cheek as he bent his head, inhaling her scent.

He turned, his lips curving into a smile that sent a shiver of pleasure down her spine as her nipples hardened. "Rianna."

His voice was a soft, coaxing siren call she couldn't resist. She took a step forward, then another, her mind screaming at her to run, but her body ignored the warnings.

Before she knew it, she was in his arms, his lips on hers, and a kiss filled with a passion that stunned her. It was wrong, but it felt so right. Her body responded, warmth spreading through her as her thoughts scattered. Her lips parted involuntarily in response. The heat of the Alpha's massive body against hers made her own betrayingly pliable. His head dipped lower, mouth covering hers in a searing kiss. Unbidden, a whimper escaped her.

He deepened the kiss, his hands sliding down her back and pulling her closer. She should fight or push him away, but she couldn't. She didn't want to.

At the thought, panic resurfaced, galvanizing her once more. Reality crashed down. This was Halox. Her enemy. Her pursuer. The man who wanted to make her his mate and subjugate her to his will.

With a surge of desperation, she tore her lips from his, her breath coming in ragged gasps. "No," she whispered, her voice filled with fear and regret.

His eyes narrowed, a dangerous glint in his lilac gaze. "You can't fight this, Rianna. You're mine."

She shook her head, tears welling in her eyes. "I won't be." She couldn't let this happen. Seizing the magic inside, she funneled it into the diversion spell she'd so painstakingly memorized. Chanting the words, she reached for the elusive magic, her desperation giving her focus and lending her strength.

This time, the magic answered in spades. A burst of energy erupted from her hands, creating a dazzling light that blinded Halox. The disorienting force sent him reeling.

The orc roared in pain and confusion, his grip on her slackening for just an instant. It was all the time Rianna needed. She wrenched free, stumbling back as tears streamed down her face. A torrent of emotions raged within her— desire, terror, guilt, and shame.

"You can't run forever." Halox's voice was a growl filled

with primal fury and dark promise. His lilac eyes fixed on her, filled with a hunger that chilled her to the bone.

"I won't be yours." Her body ached with longing, but she fought it, clutching the grimoire to her chest like a talisman.

A rueful smile twisted Halox's thick lips. "You have no choice. You were marked from the moment you were born. The magic won't let you go. *I* won't let you go."

A sob escaped her lips. She knew he was right. The mark on her neck throbbed, a constant reminder of the invisible bond that tethered her to the orc and constantly urging her to surrender, but she couldn't give in. She wouldn't.

With a cry, she turned and ran, her feet pounding against the concrete, the sound echoing in the empty tunnel, though part of her soul fractured at the self-inflicted separation. She didn't dare look back. He was behind her. She could feel him, his presence like a shadow looming over her.

She stumbled on, her heart aching with a regret she couldn't understand. Part of her wanted to stay, to surrender, but she couldn't.

Her body yearned for his, but her mind rebelled at the thought of being possessed and dominated by any creature. She had to resist the Omega pull somehow, but each encounter only increased Halox's determination, even as it further awakened her own traitorous instincts. She couldn't run forever. A reckoning was coming that could end only one of two ways—with her freedom or her surrender.

She would be free. She had to be, but the cost of that freedom weighed heavily on her, a burden she couldn't shake, and a longing she couldn't deny. Her flight continued, but the memory of that moment in the tunnel stayed with her, a haunting presence that wouldn't let her go.

CHAPTER FIVE—RIANNA

She wasn't the only one in desperate turmoil since the arrival of the creatures through the portal. Chaos reigned in the city streets as magical beings continued to flood through the breached portal. Rianna witnessed scenes of mayhem and violence as she ducked down alleys and slipped through shadows, evading the roving bands of looters.

Orc warriors rampaged unchecked, smashing storefronts, and hauling off anything of value. She watched from behind a dumpster as they whooped and cackled, adorned in their ill-gotten riches. One dragged a velvet gown through the rubble, presenting it with a roguish grin to a female orc, who swatted him playfully. Even monsters sought normalcy.

Elsewhere, a cafe owner shouted and waved a bat, trying to deter a cluster of goblins harassing his patrons. The diminutive creatures jeered and cavorted, leaping onto tables to pilfer pastries and upend mugs. One shrieked in delight at the spraying coffee, dancing with madcap energy fueled by the caffeine.

The skies too teemed with unfamiliar lifeforms. Great winged shapes soared and swooped, diving to snatch up the unwary. Rianna glimpsed a dragon's sinuous silhouette gliding between skyscrapers, drawn by the panicked crowds below. An echoing roar heralded a burst of flame, bringing screams and billowing smoke.

More unnatural howls and cries rang out from the city's darkened bowels. She saw lithe forms with glowing red eyes slipping into subways and sewers to stalk the vulnerable. Creatures of the night, flesh-hungry and ruthless. She shuddered, quickening her pace.

Even magic itself had become unreliable in the hands of nascent human users, fluctuating wildly, or exploding unexpectedly. Rianna witnessed a young woman lose control of a spell, blasting a crater in the pavement. The stunned girl stared down at her hands like they were foreign objects. Magic's resurgence wouldn't be gentle.

The city had become a pressure cooker with the tensions growing daily. It was only a matter of time before things boiled over. She soon found herself witnessing that tipping point.

It began with a brick. Cast from the hands of a scrawny human man, the brick sailed through the air, striking an unsuspecting orc squarely between the shoulder blades. He roared, whirling toward the direction from which it had come. More small projectiles pelted the group of orcs from the swelling crowd of humans. Jeers and shouts grew louder, fueling the growing hostility.

The orcs bristled, hands dropping to the cruel axes and spiked clubs at their belts. Their leader, a battle-scarred brute with a missing eye, bellowed something guttural, but his followers' blood was up. They thumped chests and brandished weapons, advancing toward the humans.

"Get out of our city, scum," yelled an angry youth, brandishing a length of pipe overhead before bringing it crunching down on an orc's armored shoulder. Dark blood dripped from the point of impact.

The leader barked another harsh command to stand down, but his warriors were beyond restraint now. More weapons emerged from the mass of orc bodies. The human crowd responded in kind, producing an arsenal of baseball bats, tire irons, and broken bottles.

A whiskey bottle exploded against the scarred orc's head. He shook his shaggy mane with a roar, fresh blood mixing with old scars. The battle-hungry orcs needed no further provocation. With guttural war cries, they charged the human line, bringing clubs and axes smashing down. The humans met them head-on, fists and weapons flying.

Rianna could only stare in dismay as bodies began to fall from the swelling violence. An orc swung a club, catching a man across the knees, dropping him as he screamed in agony. A woman swung a bat two-handed, cracking an orc's ribs before he backhanded her savagely away. This was madness.

Like sharks smelling blood, other beings were drawn to the spreading chaos. More orcs flooded in, along with packs of goblins, and some less identifiable creatures. The neighborhood became a war zone of different factions clashing and spilling each other's blood.

Rianna's heart sank at the spreading violence. This solved nothing and only bred more hatred and collective suffering. Both sides were trapped in the savage cycle, reason lost to rage. She was powerless to stop it—just one woman amid the carnage. How could she hope to restore order?

The answer came to her with chilling certainty—Halox. For all his savagery, he seemed to command the orc clans from what she'd observed while evading them. Could he restrain them and enforce order, at least among his kind?

The thought of allying with him filled her with dread, but the alternative was continued anarchy. She had to try, even if he could only control the orcs. Halox represented a starting point.

Finding privacy in a nearby office building with the foyer windows destroyed, she steeled herself before removing her shielding and warding spells. Then she whispered a summoning spell she found in the grimoire.

It didn't take long. She heard him coming before his booted feet crunched the glass from the broken windows. He appeared in the doorway, his piercing lilac eyes instinctively finding hers.

"Why do you reach out now, love?" His voice was like a low peal of thunder.

Rianna met his gaze. "The city descends into bloodshed between your warriors and the humans. Only you can restore order."

Halox weighed her words. "I hold sway only over the orc clans. For you, I'll restrain them." His eyes smoldered. "For a price. You will stand publicly as my Omega. The human women need an example to look to, and it makes sense that as Supreme General of the Orcs, it would be my mate."

Fear trickled down Rianna's spine at hearing his title, which was somehow even more intimidating than she'd expected, but she held firm. "If you stop the orcs, I'll stand with you, but the other creatures must cease as well."

Halox nodded. "I possess magic that even other Mythics must heed, though it taps my strength, and I can't use it all the time. I'll apply it, and the horde under my command, as needed, to try to keep peace. Will you take my hand freely if I end this conflict?" He extended his palm, gaze burning into hers.

Heart pounding, she reached out slowly, her small hand engulfed by his immense one. His fingers closed gently, a rumbling purr escaping him.

They left the office together, and she gasped at the sight before her. The park had become a war zone between orcs and humans. He led her to a nearby fountain, climbing atop it like it was a dais, and he was every inch the imposing warlord.

Halox raised his arms, chanting in a resonating language. The air rippled with power that pressed heavily upon every being, forcing the warring sides to their knees. Weapons fell from slack hands, and all eyes turned to the orc general.

In the magical silence, Halox drew Rianna close with one huge hand. "I give you my Mate. Let no being dare dispute this."

Rianna stood motionless as the orcs' cries echoed around her. Halox's massive hand engulfed her shoulder, holding her firmly in place at his side. To the eyes of human and Mythic alike, she was now irrefutably his.

The bargain was struck. Her freedom exchanged for a chance at peace. She searched inward for regret or bitterness but found only weary acceptance. She was tired of running, especially since part of her didn't want to escape him. She was almost excited by the turn of events that had united them.

As the stridency faded, she met Halox's strange lilac gaze. Their union was one of necessity, not choice, but they were bound by more than mere politics. His hand shifted, clawed fingers twining gently with hers.

Together, they turned to survey the kneeling throngs. Violence had been averted for now. How long this fragile order could last, she didn't know, but Halox would enforce his will on the orc clans to maintain it. Just as she must broker understanding between the Mythics and the humans. She understood her role was to be a bridge between two worlds and try to convince the human women to accept their fate. That left a bitter taste in her mouth.

Rianna felt the eyes of the other Mythics on her—the elves, giants, vampires, and countless more races brought forth through the shattered barrier. Their reactions ran the gamut from grudging acceptance to thinly veiled hostility at an outsider being elevated so highly among them, but none dared oppose Halox's raw display of power. For now, order would be kept, if uneasily. There was hope in that spark of unity.

Yet with night falling, fear and uncertainty loomed on the horizon. She shivered as she realized it was her own uncertain future that scared her most. Now that she had accepted Halox's claim, she was sure he'd want to mate with her. The thought terrified and excited her in equal measure, leaving the logical side of her horrified, but the emotional side already purring with anticipation.

Chapter Six—Halox

Halox rumbled low in his throat at the satisfaction of having his mate beside him. He'd grown weary of chasing her, but now, she was his. He gestured to his second, General Taxlos, who was still bleeding from the head, but it appeared to be a minor wound, at least for an orc. "I'm returning to base with my mate."

His general nodded. "Of course, sir."

"Keep them in line."

Taxlos looked puzzled. "The orcs?"

He shook his head, making his braids fly. "All the Mythics." He ignored Taxlos's shocked expression as he lifted Rianna and dropped her over his shoulder. He set a brisk pace back to Fort Tyron, which his clan now controlled. It was in the midst of becoming an orc stronghold.

He carried Rianna through the gates, ignoring the curious stares of his warriors. He strode directly to his tent, where he lowered her to her feet.

Rianna's cheeks were flushed, her eyes bright. "What are

you doing?"

Halox grinned. "Claiming what's mine."

She swallowed hard. "I don't think—"

"That's right," he interrupted. "Don't think. Feel." He stepped closer, towering over her. "I can smell your arousal, Rianna. Your body wants me, even if you're not ready to admit it."

She opened her mouth to protest, but he silenced her with a kiss. She melted into him, her body responding to his touch. Reluctantly, he forced himself to break the kiss and turned to a nearby guard. "Send for the mage."

Rianna looked confused, both by the kiss and him stopping, which made him smile in pleasure. She liked his touch, as she was designed to. Soon, she would accept their mating and take his cock, keeping his knot in her for hours. First...

"Why do you need a mage?"

"We must have a binding ceremony. It's an important ritual to my people." He caressed her small back with his large hand, anticipating removing her clothes one at a time and exploring the silken expanse of her light brown skin.

Her large dark eyes looked at him warily. "Do you mean, like...married?"

Despite the spell his mage had cast to allow him to understand all languages, it took his mind a moment to make the comparison. "Yes, it's very similar."

She frowned. "I'm not sure about that. We barely know each other."

He chuckled. "That's why we have the ceremony. It's to bind us magically and biologically. It's a sacred ritual, and it's necessary for us to be able to breed."

She paled. "Breed? What does that mean?"

He chuckled. "I'm certain you know what breeding means." Taking pity on her, he added, "Once the ceremony is complete, you'll immediately enter estrus, be fertile, and ready to bear my offspring."

She backed away from him, her eyes wide. "I can't have children. I'm a scientist. I have a career. I can't just drop everything to raise a family."

He shrugged. "You can still have your career. You can work in a lab here in the fort." He arched a brow as he looked around. "Though you will have to find a way to reconcile magic and science, my mate."

"Rianna," she snapped. "That's my name."

Halox laughed. "I know your name, my lovely female. I merely enjoy calling you my mate." His voice dropped an octave. "I've been pining for one all my life, and there aren't many orc females who are Omegas."

She frowned. "Aislinn told me something about Omegas and Alphas."

He nodded. "Omegas are special to our kind. They're the ones who can carry our young. They're also the only ones who can satisfy our needs."

Rianna's frown deepened. "What do you mean by that?"

"Alphas like myself need a certain type of female to accommodate us. The Omega female. Without her, we can't reproduce, and without us, the Omega female can't get pregnant. It's a symbiotic relationship."

"So, I'm an Omega, and you're an Alpha, and that's why I feel this way?"

Halox nodded. "Exactly. Our bodies recognize each other on a primal level. It's instinctual. A biological imperative." He couldn't resist cupping her breast and exploring a turgid nipple. "And it's getting harder and harder to resist."

She moaned softly, arching into his touch. "I don't know if I can do this. I've never felt like this before. It's like I'm losing control of my own body."

Halox smiled. "That's because you're an Omega. It's natural for you to want to submit to your Alpha. To give yourself over to me completely."

Rianna shivered, her body trembling with desire. "I don't

know if I can do that. It goes against everything I've ever believed in. Everything I've ever worked for."

He leaned down, his lips brushing against her ear. "You can do it. The magic and our bond compel you. I promise you, it'll be like breathing. You won't even have to think about it. It'll just happen."

Her breath hitched, her body responding to Halox's words. Her body trembled, making his cock swell as she pressed closer to him. "I don't know..."

He tried to restrain himself, knowing he couldn't claim her cunt yet. Not until the binding ceremony, and after he'd allayed her fears. "You can trust me, Rianna. I won't hurt you. I'll take care of you. I'll protect you and provide for you. All you have to do is let go and let the magic guide you."

He stopped then, because Yilax joined them. She was only one of a few female Orcs in his immediate tribe, since the birth of male orcs was nearly eight times the number of females. She was their Mage and an Alpha, so she understood the importance of this moment. Giving him a wide smile, she turned to Rianna.

"You must be the crafty human who's eluded our leader for so many days." Yilax laughed, clearly pleased.

Halox scowled at her. "That isn't a source of amusement."

Yilax tossed her green braid over her shoulder. "It is to me, brother."

Rianna's eyes widened. "Brother?"

Halox sighed. "My sister, Yilax. She's a pain in my ass."

Yilax snorted. "Only because you're too uptight. You need to relax, Halox. Have fun. Enjoy life."

Halox growled at her. "I am enjoying life. I finally have a mate."

Yilax's eyes gleamed with approval. "Ah, yes. The human. I see you've captured her. Well done, brother."

Rianna stiffened in his arms. "Captured? Is that what you call it?"

Halox stroked her hair. "Shhh, love. It's a figure of speech. I didn't capture you. I claimed you. There's a difference."

Rianna's eyes narrowed. "Not much of one, and I summoned you."

Halox sighed. "Enough. We're here to perform the binding ceremony."

Yilax nodded. "Yes, of course. I'm ready." She pulled a small pouch from her belt and removed a handful of herbs. She sprinkled them into a bowl, then added a few drops of oil before she chanted in the ancient tongue, her voice rising and falling in a hypnotic rhythm.

Rianna watched, clearly transfixed, as the mixture began to glow with a soft golden light. The glow intensified, bathing the three of them in its radiance.

Halox felt the magic gathering, swirling around and infusing them with its power. He could sense Rianna's apprehension, but he knew she was feeling the pull of the magic too. The bond between them was growing stronger, and there was no turning back now.

The light flared brighter, enveloping them in a cocoon of warmth and energy. Halox reached out, taking Rianna's hand in his. The connection between them solidified, the bond growing stronger with each passing second.

The light faded, and the magic dissipated, but the bond remained. He could feel it, a tangible thread that connected him to her. It was a powerful sensation, and she must be able to feel it too. He looked down at Rianna, seeing the wonder and awe in her eyes. She was his now, and he would cherish and protect her for the rest of their lives.

"I can't believe it," she whispered. "I can feel the bond between us. It's like nothing I've ever experienced before."

He smiled, pulling her closer. "You're mine now, love."

Rianna snuggled against his chest, sighing contentedly. "I can't believe how safe and protected I feel with you. It's like I was always meant to be yours."

His heart swelled with tenderness. "You were always meant to be mine." He kissed her forehead, inhaling her sweet scent. "And I was always meant to be yours. The magic knew what it was doing when it brought us together."

"It's still strange, especially since I'm a scientist. I don't have words for all this magical...stuff."

He smiled as he pushed aside the flap to his tent. "Come with me, my Omega. It's time to completely claim you."

She hesitated, but when he offered his hand, she grasped it. He was gratified when she clung to it and followed him into the tent.

She stopped and stared. "It's amazing. I was expecting sleeping bags or something. How did you get it to be so luxurious?"

He chuckled. "Magic, of course. I wanted to make you comfortable."

She gave him a shy smile. "Thank you. That was thoughtful."

He sat on the edge of the bed and patted the space beside him. "Sit with me, Rianna."

She perched next to him, looking nervous.

He took her hand in his, stroking it gently. "There's no need to be afraid, love. I would never hurt you."

She nodded, but he could sense her tension. He leaned in and brushed his lips against hers, tasting her sweetness. She responded to his kiss, her lips parting slightly as she sighed. He deepened the kiss, exploring her mouth with his tongue. She tasted like honey and sunshine, and he couldn't get enough of her.

He broke the kiss and gazed into her eyes, seeing the desire and longing reflected in their depths. "You're mine, Rianna. My mate. My Omega, and I'll take care of you for the rest of our lives."

She nodded, her voice barely a whisper. "I know. I can feel the bond between us. I can feel your emotions and almost sense your thoughts. It's like we're connected on a deeper level."

He smiled, tracing her jawline with his thumb. "That's the magic of the binding ceremony. It links our souls and our minds, creating a bond nothing can break."

She shivered, leaning into his touch. "It's overwhelming, but it also feels right. Like this is where I'm supposed to be. With you."

He wrapped his arms around her, pulling her close. "You're supposed to be with me. Always."

He kissed her again, his passion igniting as she responded to his touch. She was his now, and he would never let her go.

The kiss grew more heated, their tongues entwining as they explored each other's mouths. Her arousal grew, and his own desire surged in response. He broke the kiss, gazing into her eyes. "I need to claim you, to make you mine."

She nodded, her eyes dark with desire. "I need you, Halox."

He kissed her again, his hands roaming over her body, exploring every curve and valley. He gently laid her back on the bed, his hands deftly removing her stained and torn shirt. His poor little mate had been living rough on the run from him. She deserved better.

He trailed kisses down her neck, nipping at her collarbone. She moaned, arching her back as he continued his exploration of her body. He cupped her breasts, teasing her nipples with his thumbs. She gasped, her hips bucking as he pinched and rolled the sensitive buds. Her arousal was intoxicating, and his cock throbbed as it grew harder and thicker.

He moved lower, kissing and licking his way down her stomach. He paused at the waistband of her pants, looking up at her. "May I?"

She nodded, her eyes wide with anticipation.

He slowly slid her pants down, revealing her perfect, smooth skin. He groaned as he saw the wetness coating her cunt, glistening in the dim light.

"You're so beautiful, Rianna. So perfect."

He buried his face between her thighs, inhaling her scent. She was like a drug, and he was instantly addicted. He licked and sucked at her folds, savoring her taste. She writhed beneath him, moaning and gasping as he pleasured her.

He teased her clit with his tongue, circling and flicking it. She cried out, her hips bucking as he drove her closer to release. He could sense her orgasm building, and he increased his efforts, determined to bring her to the brink.

She screamed as she came, her body shuddering with pleasure. He lapped at her juices, prolonging her climax. She was exquisite, and he was captivated by her. He could spend eternity between her legs, bringing her to ecstasy over and over.

Yet being inside her beckoned with a compulsion he couldn't deny. Halox rose, looming over her. His cock was rock hard, and her eyes widened as she took in its size.

"It's so big. I don't know if it'll fit." She put her arm near his shaft, and her eyes widened further.

He understood her fear, since his member was as long as her forearm and thicker than her wrist—before he knotted. He smiled, stroking her cheek. "Don't worry, love. The magic will help you. You were made for me, and I was made for you. Our bodies will fit together perfectly."

After parting her thighs and rearranging her slightly, he positioned his shaft at her entrance, rubbing the head of his cock through her slick folds. She moaned, her hips arching toward him.

"Please, Halox, I need you."

He pressed forward, slowly easing his length into her tight channel. She gasped, her eyes widening as he stretched her. He could feel the magic working, helping her body adjust to accommodate him.

The sensation was incredible, her hot, wet walls gripping him like a vise. He groaned, fighting the urge to thrust mindlessly into her cunt. He had to take it slowly, letting her adjust to his size. He rocked his hips gently, pushing a little deeper with each stroke. She moaned, her nails digging into his shoulders as he filled her.

"You're so big. It feels so good."

He growled, his control slipping as her body yielded to him. He gripped her hips, holding her in place as he began to move faster, driving into her with increasing force. She cried out, her back arching as he pounded into her. The sound of their flesh meeting echoed through the room, mingling with her cries of pleasure.

Her inner walls clenched around him, her body quivering as she neared her peak. He gritted his teeth, fighting the urge to spill his seed yet. He wanted to savor this moment, to draw out their pleasure for as long as possible.

Her eyes flew open, gaze locking with his. "I'm going to come. I can't hold it back."

He grinned, his voice a low growl. "Then don't. Come for me, Rianna. Let me hear you scream my name."

She threw her head back, her body tensing as she came. "Yes, Halox, yes."

He roared, his knot swelling as he spilled his seed deeply inside her. The sensation was unlike anything he'd ever experienced, confirming he'd found his mate. He could have sex with another, but he could only knot and bond with his true mate. His Omega. He held her tightly, his body trembling as he kept emptying cum into her.

They laid together, still joined by his knot, basking in the afterglow of their lovemaking. Her heart beat against his chest, her breathing slowing as she drifted off to sleep. He stroked her hair, marveling at how lucky he was to have found her.

She slept for a bit, and when she woke, Rianna seemed startled. "You're still inside me."

He laughed. "I will be for a while. The knot ebbs and flows. When it softens, I'll fuck you again. We'll do this until your estrus passes. At least a week, maybe longer."

She blinked. "I can't stay here that long. I have responsibilities. A job." Her expression clouded. "I've already been gone too long with…evading you." She licked her lips as though expecting a reprimand.

He didn't bother to shame her for running. He was surprisingly proud that she'd managed to keep away from him for a week. Still, this couldn't be rushed. "I'm sorry. I know this is all new to you, but you must understand that you're my mate now. Your place is at my side. Your only responsibility is to bear my young and keep my bed warm. Besides, it's impossible to separate right now."

She struggled to sit up, wincing as his knot tugged at her. "I can't do that. I have a life. A career. I can't just abandon everything because of some stupid biological imperative."

He clenched his teeth in anger. "This isn't just some 'stupid biological imperative.' This is our destiny, and your world has changed. Your job probably doesn't exist any longer, and none of that matters anyway now. You must accept that. You should focus on practical matters, not whatever you were doing in your previous life."

"I'm a quantum physicist. I was studying the nature of reality."

Halox shrugged. "Whatever. You can study the nature of reality here. I'll even give you a lab."

Rianna gaped at him. "Are you serious?"

"Of course. Why wouldn't I be?"

She shook her head. "I don't know. I guess I thought you'd want me to be at your beck and call."

Halox snorted. "I don't care what you do, as long as you're happy, and as long as you're available to me whenever I need you, and you care for our younglings. You will soon be round with my baby. Very soon…"

Rianna frowned. "What do you mean by that?"

Halox grinned as his knot started to soften. "I mean that I

need to fuck you again. Right now."

Rianna's eyes widened as his cock hardened, pressing against her. "But I'm sore. Can't we wait a little bit?"

Halox shook his head. "No. I need to fuck you. Now."

Rianna moaned as he withdrew slightly before sliding his cock into her again, stretching her pussy. Halox grunted as he thrust into her, filling her completely. "You're so tight. You feel so good." He fucked her hard, his cock slamming into her. She moaned as he took her, her body automatically responding to his.

"I didn't think I could do this again, but..." She trailed off with a moan.

He thrust harder as the walls of her cunt clamped around his thick shaft. He was close to coming, and he could feel her getting close too.

"So good." He thrust harder, feeling her body tense as she came. He kept driving into her, his cock throbbing as he got closer and closer to his own release. Her pussy clenched around his cock as she came once more.

He thrust into her another time, his cock pulsing as he came. He groaned, twitching as he emptied his seed into her.

She laid panting beneath him, eyes closed as she enjoyed the afterglow. He stayed inside her, his cock still hard, and his knot swollen again to keep them locked together.

"I can't believe how much you can come," she murmured. "I've never felt so full."

He grinned. "I told you, I'm an Alpha. We have a lot of stamina."

She opened her eyes and looked up at him. "I can't believe I'm doing this. It's crazy."

He laughed. "I know, but it's the best thing that's ever happened to me."

She blushed. "Really?"

He nodded. "Absolutely. I've been waiting for you my whole life."

She smiled. "That's sweet."

He kissed her, his tongue exploring her mouth. She moaned, her body responding to his touch.

He cuddled and stroked her until his knot started to shrink about an hour later. She moaned, and it was hard to tell with anticipation or perhaps a little dread.

"I need to fuck you again."

"I know." She sounded resigned, but her dark eyes glowed with hunger. She gasped as he flipped her over, positioning her on her hands and knees. He entered her from behind, his cock sliding into her wet pussy.

She moaned. "You're so big this way."

He grinned as he began to thrust into her, filling her entirely. "I know. You like it though, don't you?"

She moaned, her body rocking back to meet his thrusts. "Yes. So much."

He thrust harder. She moaned and gasped, her body trembling as he took her.

"I'm going to come." She panted. "I'm going to come all over your cock."

He growled, his cock throbbing as her cunt clenched around him. "Yes. Come for me, Rianna. I want to feel you come."

She cried out, her body shaking as she came yet again. He groaned, his cock pulsing as he came too, spurting more of his seed deeper inside her. By the time her estrus finished, he wondered if either of them would be able to walk straight for at least a week.

When she finally fell asleep, and his knot softened enough to disengage, he slipped from the bed and went to the window. He wanted to give her a chance to rest, though the need to have her again was already building.

The moon was high in the sky, casting its silvery light over the landscape. The tents of his clan spread out below, and beyond them, the lights of New York City. It was a strange sight, the ancient ways of his people coexisting with the modern world.

He sighed, thinking of Rianna. She was a brave and resourceful female, but she was also stubborn and independent. She would likely resist the idea of staying with him, of becoming his mate, but the magic was strong, and the bond between them was permanent.

He turned away from the window, his gaze falling on the sleeping form of his mate. She was beautiful, her dark skin glowing in the moonlight. He smiled at the knowledge she was his, and he'd never let her go. Even now, her womb might be preparing to carry his child. It sent a primitive surge of satisfaction through him.

He climbed back into bed, pulling her close. She stirred, murmuring softly as she nestled against him. He kissed the top of her head, breathing in her scent. As his cock throbbed with renewed arousal, he knew the next few days would be challenging for her, but she would adapt and come to crave his cock. After all, she was his mate, and the magic had chosen her for him.

CHAPTER SEVEN—RIANNA

Rianna woke slowly, blinking against the sunlight filtering through the tent. For a moment, she forgot where she was, expecting to find her sparse apartment bedroom. Then awareness settled over her along with the warm weight pressed against her back.

Halox. The orc's thickly muscled arm was draped over her, holding her possessively even in sleep. His rumbling exhales stirred her hair with each breath. She laid very still, adjusting to his proximity. She was in his tent, with all the luxury fittings. Gold, jewels, and fine fabrics had transformed the space into an orcish den of indulgence.

Carefully, she shifted in the circle of his embrace. He grunted, arm tightening to pull her tighter against him. Heat radiated from his bare green skin against her back. She felt small and fragile cradled against the Alpha's immense frame, but she was no longer afraid. How could she be after the last few days of frantic mating, which had passed in a blur?

She felt different today. The sight of his naked body still

aroused her, but it didn't fill her with the same edge of need that made her think she might die if she didn't have his cock inside her for hours.

Her body felt different too. The constant ache in her belly had subsided, replaced by a sense of contentment. She felt safe and protected in Halox's arms, as if nothing could harm her. It was a strange sensation and one that she wasn't used to feeling.

She had always been a loner, relying on herself for everything. With both her parents dead and no siblings, she'd never had anyone to rely on, and she had never trusted anyone enough to let them get close to her, but now, with Halox, she knew she could trust him. She could let him take care of her, and she didn't always have to be in control. It was a strange feeling, but it was also a good one.

His eyes fluttered open, and he smiled down at her. "Good morning, love."

Rianna smiled back, unable to resist the warmth in his gaze. "Good morning."

Halox leaned in and kissed her, his lips soft and gentle against hers. She sighed, melting into the kiss. It was a far cry from the frenzied, almost violent, mating of the past few days.

Halox pulled back, his eyes searching hers. "How are you feeling?"

Rianna considered the question. "I feel...good. Better than I've felt in a long time."

His smile widened. "I'm glad to hear that. I was worried about you."

She raised an eyebrow. "You were?"

He nodded. "Of course. You're my mate, and I care about you. I want you to be happy and healthy."

Her heart warmed at his words. She had never had anyone care about her like that before, and it was a nice feeling.

His expression turned serious. "I know this is all new to you, but I hope you'll give our relationship a chance. I know we can be happy together."

Rianna hesitated, unsure what to say. She wanted to believe him, but she was still wary of trusting anyone. Everything had changed so drastically, and she still struggled to fully accept the world as it was now.

He seemed to sense her uncertainty. "I know you're scared, love, but I promise I'll take care of you. You're safe with me."

She swallowed, her throat suddenly dry. She wanted to believe him, but she had spent her entire life taking care of herself. It was hard to let go of that and trust someone else to take care of her, especially when a magical apocalypse had instigated the situation. Yet it was precisely because of that apocalypse that she was in a position to need someone to watch her back. And it was all her fault.

He stroked her hair, his touch gentle. "Just give it time. You'll see I'm telling the truth."

Rianna nodded, relaxing into his embrace. She just needed to give it time.

He kissed the top of her head. "Now, let's get you something to eat. You must be starving."

Her stomach growled as if on cue. She hadn't realized how hungry she was until he mentioned it.

Halox chuckled. "I'll take that as a yes."

He rose from the bed, and she admired the play of muscles across his broad back as he stretched. He was a magnificent specimen of masculinity, and a spark of desire surged as she watched him.

Halox glanced over his shoulder and caught her staring. He smirked, his eyes darkening with lust. "Like what you see, love?"

She blushed, looking away. "Maybe."

He chuckled, his voice low and husky. "I like the way you look at me. It makes me want to take you again."

Her blush deepened, and she felt a rush of heat between her legs. She wanted him too, but she was still sore from the previous days' activities.

He seemed to sense her hesitation as he crossed the room and knelt beside the bed, taking her hand in his. "Don't worry. I want to mate with you again, but not right away. After you eat, I want to show you my clan and introduce you."

Curiosity piqued, she nodded. "I'd like that, and I want to know more about your world. Planet? Dimension?" How did that work, with the portal opening into Earth from their world?

"I'm not sure which it is, but it's one of many—and the portal on Earth opens to them all, which is why there are more than Orcs coming through every day." He rubbed his chin, which was thick with green-black growth after their days in bed. "Like orcs, most of the other Mythics have been hoping and waiting for a way back to Earth. Our forefathers told of the harmonious and blissful days when Earth women were our subservient mates."

Her eyes narrowed. "I'm not going to be subservient to anyone."

He grinned. "You will to me, love. You're my mate, and you'll obey me in all things."

She glared at him. "I don't think so."

He laughed, his eyes twinkling with amusement. "We'll see."

His arrogance annoyed her, but she was determined to remain the woman she'd always been. She might have some magic now, and she'd had to radically adjust her worldview, but she was still someone who spoke her mind and did what she thought was right. No mate was going to change that.

Her eyes widened as she took in the scene before her. The camp was bustling with activity, with orcs and other Mythic creatures moving about. There were tents set up everywhere, and groups of orcs sparred with each other in an open field.

She spotted a group of elves practicing archery, their graceful movements mesmerizing to watch. A group of dwarves were busy crafting weapons and armor, their skilled hands working quickly. She saw a centaur sunning nearby, its horse-like body gleaming in the sunlight.

It was a fascinating glimpse into another world, and she was eager to learn more. She looked up at Halox, who was watching her with a smile on his face. "What do you think, love?"

She smiled back at him. "It's amazing. I had no idea there were so many different kinds of Mythic creatures."

Halox laughed. "There are many more than you can see here. The multiverse is a vast place, and there are many species that have yet to make contact with humans."

She nodded, her eyes wide with wonder. "I can't wait to learn more."

Halox squeezed her hand. "And you will."

She smiled up at him, her heart swelling with affection. He was a good male, and she was lucky to have him as her mate even if he was a bit arrogant.

They continued walking through the camp, and she saw a group of females gathered around a cooking fire. They were chatting and laughing, and they looked like they were having a good time.

Halox led her over to the group, and the females greeted them with smiles. "Hello, Halox. Who is this lovely creature?"

Halox smiled proudly. "This is my mate, Rianna. Rianna, this is my sister, Lirra."

Lirra smiled warmly at Rianna. "It's a pleasure to meet you, Rianna. Welcome to the family."

She returned the smile, though she was a little unsettled to be identified as orc family so casually. "Thank you. It's nice to meet you too." She looked at Halox. "You didn't tell me you had two sisters."

He shrugged. "It didn't occur to me to mention."

Lirra rolled her eyes as the other females laughed at Rianna's snort of reaction. Then the other females introduced themselves, and she was surprised to find they were all friendly and welcoming. She had expected them to be standoffish or resentful of her, but they seemed genuinely happy for Halox.

Lirra took Rianna's arm. "Come, let me show you around the camp."

She nodded, glancing back at her mate.

"Go ahead, love. I'll catch up with you later."

Rianna allowed Lirra to lead her away, and the two women chatted as they walked. Lirra was curious about Rianna's life on Earth, where she was now living, and Rianna was curious too.

"Did you come to Earth because you had to? I mean, did the portal opening suck your here?" asked Rianna.

Lirra shook her head. "No. We've had centuries watching for an age, always hoping it would open again. We require mates."

Her eyes widened. "You're seeking human females too?"

Lirra blinked before shaking her head, making her moss-green hair fly around her face. "Some have that inclination, but we must have a partner of the opposite biological designation to reproduce. Only an Alpha can breed with an Omega to produce offspring. Some human males will be Omegas too. There are too many Alphas and not enough Omegas among the Mythics."

"So, you need to breed with us? But you're not human." As a scientist, the idea of such disparate species being compatible was mindboggling.

"No, but our ancestors were compatible. Long ago, our worlds were connected, and our people mingled freely, but something happened, and the portals between our worlds closed. We returned to our homeworld but were unable to access Earth. It's a great mystery."

She hesitated, knowing exactly how the portal had closed,

thanks to Aislinn's information. It didn't seem prudent to admit to the Alpha orc female that human women and magic users had collaborated to lock them out.

"I see. So, you've been waiting for the portal to reopen?"

"Yes, and it has. We can finally return to Earth and claim our mates. With so few Omegas among us, not many have managed to reproduce. Now, all the Alphas can finally have the families we've been denied for so long."

Rianna's eyes widened as she realized the implications of what Lirra was saying. "What about the humans you're planning to mate with? We have...had...lives and possibly other partners before your return."

Lirra shrugged. "They will be given a choice. If they choose to stay with their current partners, we will respect that, but if they choose to leave their old lives behind and become our mates, we will provide for them and protect them for the rest of their lives."

Rianna frowned. "You all believe in giving a choice?" She recalled Aislinn mentioning a lot of Alphas took what they wanted when they'd roamed the Earth a thousand years ago.

"Most of us do. There are those who don't, but there's something wrong with them." She spoke with quiet conviction. "They don't interpret the biological imperative the way a true Alpha does. Our job is to protect and care for our mate, and to ensure his happiness. An Omega is what gives us meaning and purpose. To hurt our mate is unthinkable to a true Alpha."

"But if your mate doesn't want to be with you, then what?"

"Then we must accept that and move on. It's a difficult thing, but it's better than forcing a mate to be with us. That would only bring misery to both parties."

Rianna nodded, thinking of Aislinn and the others. She wondered how many Alphas would be willing to let their chosen mate go if they didn't want to be with them. She hoped Lirra was right, but she feared the possibility. If these Mythics had been denied mates for centuries, how many would be desperate from loneliness? How many would view themselves as having superior strength that gave them the right to take what they wanted?

"I'm sorry. I didn't mean to upset you," said Lirra, misinterpreting her silence.

Rianna shook her head. "I'm not upset. I'm just thinking."

"About what?"

"About the future. About what this means for me and Halox. I'm not sure what to expect, and I'm a little nervous."

Lirra smiled. "I understand. It's a big change, and you're going to have to adjust to a lot of new things, but Halox is a good male, and he'll take care of you. I know he seems a bit gruff, but he has a soft heart. He'll do anything for you."

Later, Halox arrived to collect Rianna from the females' gathering. She bid Lirra and the others farewell, promising to visit again soon.

As they walked through the camp, he kept one muscular arm wrapped firmly around her waist. His body language made it clear she belonged to him. Rianna shifted uncomfortably but didn't protest. This possessiveness was part of his nature.

When a young male orc's gaze lingered too long on Rianna, Halox snarled, yanking her tighter against him. The other orc immediately lowered his eyes in submission.

"She's mine." Halox growled at the boy, flashing his fangs. "No other dares look upon my mate."

Her temper flared. She understood Halox feeling protective, but this seemed excessive. "I don't belong to you." She pulled away enough to glare up at him. "You don't control who looks at me."

His eyes widened in surprise, then narrowed. For a moment, she thought he would lash out, but he took a deep breath, mastering himself. "Forgive me, love. I forget sometimes your ways are not ours." His voice was tight, but sincere. "Mating with you will be different than with my own kind, were I lucky enough to find an Omega."

Rianna relaxed slightly, appeased. She knew change wouldn't come quickly or easily to either of them. "I know you want to protect me," she said gently, "But I don't need sheltering from every little thing."

He looked thoughtful. "I'll try to remember." He drew her into his arms, his touch unexpectedly tender. She let her cheek rest against the warmth of his chest, encouraged by a glimpse of the sensitive male beneath the brutish warrior exterior. With time and patience, perhaps real understanding could grow between them.

Over the next few days, Rianna continued exploring the camp and learning more about Halox's world. Each new encounter was an opportunity to expand her horizons. She spent many hours talking with Lirra and the other females. Their insights helped her better understand the culture in which she now found herself immersed. They explained mating customs, social hierarchies, even fashion and cuisine unique to their people.

In turn, Rianna told them about Earth and human societies. The females were intrigued by the advanced technology and innovations she described. At times, their different values caused debate, but they learned much from each other. She was surprised to feel at home among them and started to count many, especially Lirra, as friends.

The day had been long, and tensions were running high in the war camp. Skirmishes with the centaurs along the border of the fort had left a trail of casualties on both sides. Halox had been meeting with his commanders for hours, strategizing their response.

When the war chiefs emerged, they were spoiling for revenge. One pounded a fist against his chest plate, shouting, "We should raid their encampment at dawn and slaughter them in their sleep before they can regroup."

The others bellowed their approval, but she noticed Halox remained silent, his brow furrowed. Perhaps he was less certain. If she could persuade him to choose a diplomatic solution instead of attacking, it could prevent an all-out war. There was already enough strain on the people of her world that they didn't need to add open conflict to the equation.

She waited until the last chief had departed before she turned to Halox. "Raiding the centaurs will only breed more hate and violence. Let's try to negotiate a peace treaty first."

Halox scowled, pride seemingly stung that she would question his command. "You dare interfere in matters of war?"

Rianna stood firm. "I speak because I want you to succeed, but not through reckless sacrifice."

His jaw tightened, visibly angry by her challenge to his authority. For a moment she thought he might shout at what he perceived as her insolence, but he took a slow breath, his clenched fists gradually relaxing. "You overstep your bounds." Yet there was restraint in his tone rather than real anger.

Rianna stood her ground, holding his gaze.

His shoulders loosened marginally in concession. "Your counsel has merit. I'll...consider it."

It was a small victory, but an important step. She inclined her head respectfully before leaving him to ponder her words in private. It took great strength for a warrior like him to stay calm in the face of public dissent.

As the days passed, she gathered her courage to gently contradict Halox in other instances too, asserting her right to an opinion. Each time, his initial reaction was offended anger, but he swiftly mastered himself, hearing her out, and bit by bit, he came to accept her independence even if he rarely took her thoughts into consideration. It was a slow, frustrating process, but she persisted.

One night, after a raucous celebration following a tentative truce with Caius, the leader of the Centaurs, Halox clearly expected her to remain by his side, but weariness dragged at her bones. He frowned in concern. "You're tired, love. The night grows long, and if you wish to retire to our tent, I'll escort you."

She nodded, expecting him to want to mate. Even as tired as she was, she wasn't opposed to the idea. Instead, to her surprise, he pulled her tightly against him and just held her. She was nearly asleep when he spoke.

"Your assessment was correct." He sounded almost grudging.

She blinked open her eyes. "What assessment?"

"That peace is more productive than war, especially under the current circumstances. Caius might not keep his word, but it's better not to have to fight a war with the centaurs while remaining vigilant to the other creatures and adapting to this world."

She patted his hand. "Thanks for admitting it. I figured you wouldn't say anything about my idea for peace talks and just take credit."

He grunted. "I'm an orc and a general. Taking credit for others' ideas is beneath me."

"Even a female's?"

He grunted again. "Females have equal merit. You find yourself shielded and protected because you're an Omega, not because you're female."

She started to argue but hesitated. The female Alpha orcs

fought alongside the men, and Lirra and Yilox both had high standing. It was a bitter pill to swallow to be treated as inferior because of a magical change to her reproductive system, not solely because she was female—not that she appreciated being treated that way for any reason. "Omega or not, I should have equal standing and input too."

His grunt wasn't illuminating about his opinion, but he pressed a kiss to her temple. "Sleep, love."

She let her eyes close, but only because she was exhausted, not because he'd told her to do something. The Omega in her compelled her to follow his commands, but the independent woman she'd always been refused to surrender to that biological imperative without a hell of a fight.

CHAPTER EIGHT—RIANNA

A few weeks later, Rianna stirred awake, a wave of nausea turning her stomach. She swallowed hard, willing it to pass. The sickness came most mornings now and was a reminder of the precious life growing within her.

Halox's child. Theirs. The tangible proof of the bond fate had forged between them. She placed a hand over her still-flat belly, filled with wonder and trepidation. So much change was coming that she could scarcely comprehend it.

The orc healer who examined her had confirmed the pregnancy last week after she'd scavenged a pregnancy test from a pharmacy that had been mostly looted. Halox was away leading his warriors and meeting with other Mythic leaders, so she'd kept the news to herself until his return. She smiled, imagining his reaction. The fierce orc chieftain had a tender side few saw, one that would melt at the revelation.

Voices sounded outside, along with heavy footsteps and grunts. She rose, smoothing her clothes self-consciously as her senses stirred. It was something she couldn't explain scientifically but was part of the bond. She immediately knew he was in her vicinity. Moments later, the tent flaps parted, and he ducked inside. His piercing lilac eyes found hers, and she read the depth of his longing in them. They had spent too many nights apart.

He crossed the space between them in three long strides, sweeping her into his embrace. She sighed, leaning into that powerful frame. This was home. She might not have chosen him, but she could no longer envision a life without this complex, passionate male by her side.

Halox drew back, studying her intently. "Something is different, love. Your scent..." He inhaled deeply, brows furrowing. Then his gaze sharpened. "You carry my child." He beamed in pleasure.

Rianna smiled up at him. "I wanted to tell you in person. Our family grows."

Emotion transformed his harsh features. He dropped to one knee before her, reverent hands cradling her abdomen. "Precious gift," he said, blinking heavily. "For this, I would conquer the world itself."

Her heart swelled. She gently stroked his braided hair, marveling at the depths of tenderness her gruff warrior could show when they were alone. He would be a devoted father, she had no doubt.

In the days that followed, Halox's protectiveness increased tenfold. He tended Rianna himself, bringing her choice morsels and recruiting humans to provide electricity to their encampment. He claimed it was for her comfort, but she didn't miss the way he liked to lounge in front of the air conditioning unit a clever HVAC tech had mounted on a support structure and installed in the tent.

Her body changed as well, subtle but unmistakable signs of pregnancy growing with each day. Nausea faded, but strange cravings emerged for meat and minerals. Her senses grew keener, and she could now detect his scent from afar. Most startling was an intensifying preoccupation with her Alpha—his touch, his smile, and his approval.

Pregnancy was awakening ancient Omega instincts she'd never imagined possessing. The drive to nurture their child made her more attuned to his needs as well. When he returned weary from settling disputes, she eased his off armor with caring hands. His rumbling purr was reward enough.

Yet even cocooned in Halox's doting care, Rianna didn't forget the world outside. Each day, more desperate humans camped around them, or large groups trooped out of the city, carrying what meager possessions they had as they fled the violence and upheaval. Few Mythics bothered to bring any of their own resources when they emerged from the portal, and there was still a sizable influx daily through the portal. Provisions were scarce, and the humans bore the brunt of shortages.

One morning, Rianna ventured from the tent, Lirra shadowing protectively. A group of humans had set up on the very outskirts of the orc territory, and it was causing some dissent among the orcs. She observed the newcomers' exhausted, pinched faces with growing concern. "We have to do something for them, Lirra. I might have little sway, but there are still steps we can take."

Lirra gave her a measuring look before nodding. "There are many who want to force them to continue on, but I see the children..." She trailed off with a longing look, her gaze resting on a pregnant woman. "We must protect the young of all species. It's the way of an Alpha."

"I'm glad you agree." Together, they gathered supplies—food, medicine, and blankets. Rianna approached the families at the edge of camp. "For your children," she said gently. The spark of renewed hope in their eyes warmed her, though she still worried about them. She resolved to change what small parts of this broken world she could.

She offered a jar of orc healing ointment, infused with herbs and magic, to a human man with an infection on his leg. He looked feverish and ill, but he had enough strength to slap it from her hand.

"Get that away from me. I don't want anything from them or you. Traitor." He almost spat the word at her before reeling backward and limping away.

She blinked, stunned by the venom in his rejection, but she understood too. He saw her as a traitor for siding with the monsters who had invaded their world. All she could do was persist in showing compassion.

Lirra growled at him, hand on her axe. "Should I remind him of his manners, sister?"

She snorted. "No, of course not. Let's just continue handing out what we can."

That evening, when Halox returned, she shared her activities. His expression grew troubled. "You mustn't wander so freely, not while carrying my heir. There are dangers."

Rianna lifted her chin. "I can't stand idle when people suffer. Our child deserves to grow up in a more just world."

He looked reluctant, but her determined stare brooked no argument. Finally, he dipped his head in concession. "Very well, but you will take an escort. I feel better knowing you're protected."

"Lirra was with me." She squeezed his hand. "We want the same things, my Alpha. We just see different paths to get there."

His eyes softened, a rumble of affection escaping him. With a purr, he picked her up and carried her to the bed, where he made love to her with extreme thoroughness. There was no knotting with her being pregnant, but this was just as satisfying in a different way.

Over the ensuing weeks, Rianna ventured out frequently with Lirra as escort and Yilax, who could sometimes heal with magic or alleviate anguish. None of them had the ability to conjure food. That was a limitation she'd been disappointed to learn magic couldn't evade.

She was returning to the camp one afternoon when a group of centaurs galloped into view. The orcs guarding the perimeter raised their weapons, but the leader held up a hand. "We come in peace. We seek to parley."

Halox stepped forward, his face impassive. "Speak."

The centaur bowed his head. "I am Tavros, son of Caius. My group has just arrived, and we ask to shelter here while we gather resources."

His brow furrowed as he considered the request. "I have no quarrel with your people. We have a treaty. You may shelter here if you wish."

Tavros nodded gratefully. "Thank you, General."

Rianna watched them gallop away and turned to him, outraged anew. "They bring nothing with them from their own realms. None of the Mythics do. They're taking all the resources, and my people are suffering. We have to do something."

His eyes flashed to a more vibrant purple. "What would you have me do, love? I can't make them bring supplies, and I can't make them share what they have. That's their choice."

"You can set an example. You can show them that sharing

is the right thing to do."

His jaw tightened. "I won't beg for scraps like a dog. I am a proud orc, and I won't lower myself to such ignominy."

Rianna's temper flared. "So, you would rather watch innocent people starve? You would rather let children go hungry?"

Halox's eyes narrowed. "You go too far. I won't be lectured like a child. I am the Supreme General of the entire orc army, and my decisions are final."

Rianna glared at him. "You're making a mistake. You're letting your pride get in the way of doing what's right."

Halox's eyes flashed with anger. "I have heard enough. You won't speak to me in such a manner again. Do you understand?"

Rianna's eyes blazed with fury. "Fine. I'll do what I can to help the humans, with or without you."

She stormed off, leaving Halox fuming in her wake, but she was pissed enough not to care and squashed the irritating Omega instinct that encouraged her to apologize to her mate and earn his forgiveness. Screw that.

The next day, Rianna set out once more with Lirra and Yilax to distribute supplies to the humans. It was getting more difficult to scavenge any, and they were discussing taking a trip into other parts of the city not under the orcs' control. The other Mythics had carved out their territories, but there were some unclaimed areas. It was a calculated risk that Yilax and Rianna were all for, but Lirra was against.

"You can't risk yours and the baby's safety, sister."

"I'm not helpless. I'm not going to sit here and do nothing when I know I can help."

Lirra looked at her with a mixture of admiration and exasperation. "You're a stubborn one, aren't you?"

Rianna smiled. "I've been told that a few times."

Yilax chuckled. "You fit in well with us, Rianna."

As they were walking, they came across a group of humans huddled together. They were dirty and thin, and their clothes were ragged. Rianna's heart went out to them.

"Here, take these." She held out a bag of food and water.

The humans eyed her suspiciously but eventually accepted the offering. "Thank you," said one of them quietly.

Rianna nodded and continued on her way.

"You're a good human, Rianna," said Lirra softly.

"I'm just trying to do what's right." Seeing people in these dire circumstances nearly crippled her with guilt, because her refusal to listen to Aislinn had caused this. Yet she couldn't regret having found Halox, even if he was a stubborn, barbaric, infuriating…

They continued their journey, helping as many people as they could. As the day wore on, Rianna's energy began to flag.

"Are you all right?" asked Lirra, concerned.

"I'm fine. Just a little tired."

"Maybe we should head back to camp."

Rianna nodded, feeling lightheaded. "Yeah, I think that's a good idea."

As they made their way back, her vision started to blur. She stumbled, and Lirra caught her before she could fall.

"Rianna? What's wrong?"

"I don't know, I just feel really weak all of a sudden."

Yilax touched her brow, muttering a spell. Her eyes widened, and she said, "Someone has cast a spell on Rianna."

"Who would do such a thing?" Lirra looked around as if she expected the culprit to be lurking to see their handiwork.

"I don't know, but we need to get her back to the camp and find Halox. He needs to know about this."

They hurried back to the camp, Rianna's condition worsening with each passing moment. By the time they reached the gates, she was struggling to stay conscious.

He was waiting for them, his face etched with worry. "I sensed her distress. What happened?"

"Someone cast a spell on Rianna. She's been weakened."

Halox's eyes blazed with fury. "Who did this?"

"We don't know, but we need to figure out a way to reverse the spell."

He scooped her into his arms, cradling her close. "I won't let anything happen to you, love. I swear it."

She clung to him, feeling safe in his embrace despite the lingering anger between them. "I know, Halox. I trust you."

Lirra and Yilax accompanied them to Yilax's tent, where Halox laid Rianna on a cot. She had faith in their clan's mage to find a counterspell, and his sister was soon beside her.

"Drink this," said Yilax in a soothing tone. "It will help restore your strength."

Rianna obeyed, swallowing the potion. It tasted bitter, but she could feel its effects almost immediately. Her head cleared, and she sat up, feeling more alert.

"Thank you, Yilax."

The female smiled. "Of course, Rianna. I'm glad I could help."

Halox's face was grim. "A human must have done this. You were amongst them all day."

Rianna shook her head. "I don't think so. The humans I met today were grateful for our help. I don't think any of them would have tried to hurt me, and I haven't seen that many who've gained any real control over magic yet."

"Then it must have been one of the other Mythic races," said Lirra.

Rianna frowned. "But why would they do that? I haven't had any dealings with any of the other races."

"Perhaps they're afraid of what you represent," said Yilax. "You're an Omega, and you're mated to the general. They might see you as a threat to their power."

"Or maybe it's another human like that one you

encountered," said Lirra.

"What human?" asked Halox in a low tone.

She frowned repressively at her guard. "It's been a while, but there was a man who refused help and called me a traitor." Putting a hand on his arm as he got rigid, she said, "That was all there was to it. I never felt threatened and haven't seen him again."

Halox's jaw worked, but he nodded. "I won't tolerate anyone harming you."

Rianna smiled at him. "I know, my Alpha. I'm safe with you."

He wrapped his arms around her, pulling her closer. She rested her head against his chest, breathing in his familiar scent.

"I promise to build you a throne of bones from whomever tried to hurt you." He snarled as he told her that.

Rianna wasn't entirely sure how to take that offer. She settled for a smile and said, "That's…thoughtful."

He kissed the top of her head. "I'll keep you and our child safe. I swear it."

She believed him. "I know you will." The experience had rattled her, reminding her she needed to spend more time studying the grimoire and developing her own magic to ensure no one could cast a spell on her again. In the meantime, she was glad to have the warrior on her side.

He smiled, his lilac gaze softening. "Good. Now rest. You need your strength."

Without protest, she closed her eyes, feeling safe and secure in her Alpha's arms.

Rianna woke to his gentle touch. He was stroking her hair, his expression tender.

"How are you feeling, love?"

"Better, thanks to you and Yilax."

"I'm glad." He leaned down and pressed a kiss to her forehead. "Yilax tells me that when she scanned you for a spell, she noticed your magic is much stronger. She thinks it's because of pregnancy, and the changes it's making to your body. You're a full Omega now, which makes you more receptive to using magic."

Rianna's eyes widened. "Really?"

Halox nodded. "Yes. It seems our child is already changing you, even before they're born." He smiled. "I'm proud of you. You're strong and brave. You have the heart of an orc."

Rianna blushed at the praise. "I'm just doing what I think is right."

His smile faded. "I'm sorry I didn't listen to you before. You were right, and I was wrong. I should have listened to you, and I should try to convince the other Mythic leaders to bring resources from their world, even if it's only enough for their own people."

Rianna's eyes widened. "You mean it?"

Halox nodded. "Yes. It's not fair to expect the humans to provide everything for us. We need to do our part, or it will breed more resentment. I won't have anyone targeting my mate again, so I'll remove any motivations for them to do so."

She didn't know if he'd be able to pull off such a monumental task, but she threw her arms around his neck, hugging him tightly. "Thank you for listening to me."

He hugged her back, his arms wrapped around her waist. "I'm sorry it took me so long to see the truth, but I promise I'll do better from now on."

Rianna pulled back and looked up at him, her eyes shining with happiness. "Thank you."

Halox's eyes softened, and he leaned down and captured her lips in a tender kiss. She melted into the embrace, her heart swelling with love for her Alpha. The word flickered through her mind, causing a small surge of alarm at the thought of falling in love with him, but it faded as his mouth grew more demanding.

She surrendered to his touch, her body responding to his as it always did. Her breasts tingled, and her pussy grew slick with arousal. He growled, his hands roaming over her curves. "I need you, love."

She moaned, arching into his touch. "I need you too, Halox."

He wasted no time in stripping her of her clothing, his hands exploring every inch of her naked skin. She shivered with pleasure, her nipples pebbling under his touch. He cupped her breasts, squeezing them gently while his thumbs brushed against the sensitive brown peaks.

She gasped, her hips bucking against him. He was already hard, his cock straining against his trousers. She reached for him, wanting to feel his bare skin against hers. She tugged at the laces, freeing his erection. He groaned, his head dropping back as she stroked his length.

"Fuck, love. Your touch feels so good."

She smiled, continuing her ministrations. He was thick and heavy in her hand, and his skin was hot and smooth. She ran her thumb over the tip, spreading the bead of precum that had gathered there. He shuddered, his breath coming in harsh pants.

"I need to be inside you, love."

She didn't hesitate, spreading her legs wide to accommodate him. He positioned himself between her thighs, his cock pressing against her entrance. She moaned as he slid into her, stretching and filling her in the most delicious way.

He paused, giving her time to adjust to his size. Then he began to move, thrusting in and out of her with slow, steady strokes while his fingers found her clit. The combination of his cock sliding in and out of her and his fingers rubbing her swollen bud was exquisite.

She writhed beneath him, lost in the sensations. "More, my

Alpha. I need more."

He growled, his pace increasing. She cried out as he drove into her, his thick cock hitting all the right spots. The pressure inside her built until she was teetering on the edge of release.

"Come for me, love. Come for me and milk my seed from my cock."

She shattered, her orgasm crashing over her in waves of pleasure. She screamed his name, her body trembling with the force of it. He roared as he followed her over the edge, his cock pulsing inside her as he spilled his seed. Though she missed his knot, the sensation of his cum flooding her was still incredibly satisfying.

He collapsed on top of her, his weight pinning her to the bed. She didn't mind, enjoying the closeness. She trailed her fingers along his spine, tracing the muscles of his back. He purred contentedly, nuzzling her neck.

"I love you, love," he murmured.

Her eyes widened as her heart skipped a beat. "You do?" She frowned. "Perhaps you're just confusing hormones, or the biological imperative..."

He lifted his head, his gaze fierce. "No. I love you, Rianna. I love you for your strength, your courage, and your compassion. I love you for the way you challenge me and make me a better male." His hand cupped her mound. "I love you for your wet cunt that always welcomes me, and your sweet, round ass that begs for my cock."

She laughed. "You have a way with words."

His eyes gleamed. "I have many ways with words, love, and I intend to show you them all."

She grinned. "You're not tired?"

He smirked. "Never."

She sighed happily as he proceeded to demonstrate his stamina.

The next day, Halox announced that the orcs would begin bringing supplies from their realm through the portal. The other Mythic leaders grumbled, but he was adamant. He also declared that the orcs would start distributing the resources to the humans and other Mythics in need. Rianna stood by his side, proud of him.

The other Mythic leaders agreed, albeit reluctantly, and the first shipment of goods from the orc realm arrived. The humans were wary at first but were soon lining up to receive their share of the bounty.

Rianna smiled as she watched the scene unfold. It was just the beginning, but it was a step toward peaceful coexistence, assuming the other Mythic races followed through on their agreement. As welcome as the shipment from the orc world was, it wasn't enough to alleviate all the suffering. They couldn't do that alone.

CHAPTER NINE—RIANNA

In under a week, the generous delivery of orc supplies was gone, handed to everyone who came to Ft. Tyron, be they Mythics or humans. Some humans refused to eat the orcs' offerings, which included fruits and vegetables that were unfamiliar and strange, but others were more pragmatic.

Rianna was pleased that many of the orcs had gone to their realm to hunt. The first hunting party returned with enormous gray creatures they called 'elk,' dragging them through the portal. The orcs had already skinned and butchered most, and the smell of cooking meat soon filled the air.

She was watching the orcs butcher the orc-elk when she heard a commotion. Turning, she saw a group of centaurs arguing with the orcs.

"What's going on?" she asked Lirra.

"The centaurs are demanding a larger share of the food. They say they have more mouths to feed because they brought their families with them."

Rianna frowned. "That's not fair. The orcs are providing the food, and humans are the ones who need it the most. The centaurs should go back to their realm and bring their own supplies."

Lirra shrugged. "I agree, but it's not my place to say."

The argument between the orcs and centaurs escalated, and it looked like it was about to turn into a fight. Rianna stepped forward, determined to intervene.

"Stop. This is ridiculous. We can't let this petty squabbling get out of hand. There's enough food for everyone. We just need to work together and figure out a way to distribute it fairly."

The centaurs looked at her with disdain. Tavros, Caius's son, spoke. "And what do you know of such things, human? You're just an Omega, and an orc Omega at that. You're not even worthy of being here."

Rianna bristled at his insult. "Earth is my home. I have more right to be here than any of you do. I was born here, and I'm willing to fight to protect it."

Tavros snorted. "You? Fight? I doubt that very much. You're nothing but a weak, pathetic female, and you're not worth my time. Come on, men. Let's leave this place. We'll find somewhere else to settle."

The centaurs turned, and anger surged inside her. The spells she'd memorized with her eidetic memory swirled through her mind until one for transfiguration rose to the forefront. In her anger, and with her magic bolstered by the Omega hormones flooding her body, the spell felt effortless as she recited it.

As the last syllable left her lips, a bright flash of light filled the air, and the centaurs were transformed into donkeys. The orcs roared with laughter, and the humans stared in shock. Rianna was stunned by her own power, but it was quickly replaced by anger at the centaurs' arrogance.

"You see? This is what happens when you disrespect an orc Omega. I might not be a warrior, but I can defend myself."

The centaurs brayed indignantly, but there was nothing they

could do. They were stuck in their new forms. Tavros glared at her, but he couldn't speak.

Rianna looked at the orcs. "We need to figure out a way to distribute the food fairly. Humans are the ones who are suffering the most, and we need to make sure they get the resources they need."

The orcs nodded, and Rianna knew she had their support. She looked at the humans and saw a mixture of emotions on their faces—shock, awe, and respect.

"We can't let this happen again," she said as Caius ran toward them, his hooves tearing gouges in the park land around them. She squared her shoulders to face off with the angry father and leader of the centaurs.

Caius reared up on his hind legs, his front hooves pawing the air. "What have you done to my son?"

Rianna looked at him calmly. "I turned your son and his men into donkeys, and I'll do the same to you if you don't agree to cooperate. I'm sick and tired of your kind thinking you can just take whatever you want without caring about the consequences. You're not the only ones who are suffering, and we need to work together to make sure everyone has what they need."

Caius snorted, stamping his feet. "You dare threaten me, human? I am a centaur, and you are nothing but a lowly human. You have no right to tell me what to do."

Rianna's temper flared as the words of another spell came to her. She recited it, and Caius was instantly transformed into a frog. The orcs cheered as the centaurs brayed, and their leader croaked in dismay. Rianna looked at Halox, and he nodded in approval.

"You are a true orc, Rianna. You have the heart of a warrior, and I am proud to call you my mate."

She smiled with pride and a sense of accomplishment. She had never imagined herself standing up to the Mythic invaders, but she was glad she had. She had shown them humans weren't to be trifled with, and she had made sure the orcs would be on the humans' side.

A touch of fear sent a chill down her spine. "They're going to be angry when I change them back."

Her mate chuckled. "If. They clearly understand us, so they can agree to a compromise or remain as they are. I suspect they'll choose to return to their natural form."

She smiled at the thought of the arrogant centaurs being forced to negotiate with her. "I hope they do. I don't want to have to keep turning them into animals." She pulled a face. "The sheer amount of dung involved would be unpleasant to manage."

Halox laughed, and she basked in the sound of it. Their relationship had changed since the attack on her, and she had a feeling it was a permanent shift for the better.

The next day, Halox stood beside her as they faced the angry group of donkeys, and the sole frog perched on Tavros's head. "I'm sure you've had time to consider the situation. Will you cooperate, or do we need to continue this discussion in your current state?"

Tavros nodded, and Rianna, after a moment of panic when her first attempt didn't work, and she feared they'd be trapped like this, released the spell. The centaurs shimmered with a golden glow, and then they were back in their original forms.

Caius was the first to speak, his voice deep and commanding. "I apologize for our behavior. We were wrong to assume we could take what we wanted without regard for others. We will work with the humans to make sure everyone gets what they need."

His son glared at him. "Father, how can you—"

"Silence." Caius's sharp command cut him off. "I won't tolerate such insolence. You and your men will do as I say, or you will be banished back to our realm with no hope of finding a mate."

Tavros's eyes widened, and he bowed his head in submission. "Yes, Father. I will do as you say." His gaze flicked to Rianna, hatred burning in his eyes. "But I will never forgive you for this humiliation."

Rianna shrugged. "I don't care. All I care about is making sure that everyone has what they need to survive."

Halox wrapped an arm around her waist, pulling her close. "My mate speaks the truth. We must work together if we're to survive in this world."

Caius nodded. "I agree. We will help the humans and the other races, and in return, we'll share in the bounty of this realm."

Rianna stiffened. "My world isn't just for you to pillage, Caius. You must treat it with respect, or you'll lose all chance of being welcomed here and finding mates."

Halox squeezed her shoulder reassuringly. "We'll do what we can to preserve this world, but we can't guarantee it will remain unchanged. We are Mythics, and we do what we must to survive, my mate."

Caius inclined his head toward her. "I understand. We will do our best to honor this agreement and help the orcs ensure the other races accept and contribute to the supplies. We have a treaty, and we'll uphold it."

Rianna relaxed, knowing that was the best they could do. "Thank you. I appreciate your cooperation."

Halox nodded. "I'm glad we were able to come to an understanding." His gaze swept over the group, landing on Tavros. "However, if any of you violate the treaty, there will be severe consequences. Do you understand?"

Tavros nodded, his eyes flashing with anger. "Yes, General. We understand."

"Good. Now, let's get to work."

Rianna smiled and leaned into Halox's embrace even

though she didn't miss the ugly look on Tavros's face as he glared at her. It seemed she had made an enemy, but she wasn't worried. She had Halox and the rest of the orcs on her side, and that was all that mattered.

Her mate called another meeting in Central Park. Yalix summoned the leaders of the other Mythics, making them appear. The threat of Halox's power over them was enough to make them stay, but Rianna sensed the resentment among the vampires, fae, elves, and the others.

Halox's booming voice echoed across the park. "We are gathered here today to discuss the future of this world. Earth offers the chance for Omegas, which entices all races. That means more and more come through the portals, and our numbers grow. That's good, because it means we have a greater chance of surviving and thriving here, but we must be careful. There are limited resources, and we must learn to share if we are to coexist."

A murmur of dissent rippled through the crowd, and Halox's eyes flashed with anger. "Don't test me. I am the general of the great orc army, and I have defeated countless enemies. I expect every group to contribute to communal supplies, delivered from your home worlds. If your populations are like mine, most are here now, so you have resources not being utilized in your realms. Bring them through the portal and help distribute them to the humans and other races."

The grumbling was louder, but his powerful presence kept it moderate. "I know some of you don't believe non-Omega humans deserve this consideration, but they're a part of this world, and they have suffered greatly from our arrival. You expect to find mates among them, but I don't believe the Omegas will be receptive if our presence causes suffering and misery to them and their families."

A large troll, bigger than Halox by several feet, stepped forward. "We'll take who and what we want. We don't need your permission."

Rianna's mate smiled, but there was no humor in it. "I know you think that, but I'm telling you, it's a mistake. The humans have their own weapons, and they'll use them against us. They won't hesitate to attack if they feel threatened."

The troll scoffed. "Humans? They're weak and feeble. They're nothing compared to us."

"You're wrong," said Rianna, stepping forward. "We might be weaker physically, but we have the advantage of numbers. And we have weapons that can destroy you in an instant."

The troll looked at her with contempt. "You? A puny human female?" He chortled. "Don't you recall what happened when your planes tried to bomb us? Nothing but a few injuries. You're nothing but insects to us."

Rianna's gaze hardened as she recalled the incident he'd mentioned, when the president ordered jets to attack the creatures in Central Park. It had caused damage to the land but little harm to the Mythics. "I'm not talking about human weapons, though we've barely dipped into our arsenal. Our first goal will be to keep the planet habitable, but I assure you, humans are ruthless enough to destroy everything if it kills our enemies."

"And what do you know of this?"

"I'm a scientist. I helped build the supercollider that opened the portal. It's capable of creating a black hole that could swallow all of New York City, and all of you." She squared her shoulders. "I could dedicate my time to closing the portal and keeping you all out again, but I don't need to do that." Never mind that she didn't think it was possible, based on Aislinn's information. They didn't need to know that. "Your return has brought magic back to our world, and I'll use it to defend myself and those I love. So will the other Omegas. We're not helpless, and we won't let you take what you want without a fight."

"You wouldn't dare. You're just an Omega. You're weak and powerless." The troll sneered at her.

"I'm an Omega, but I'm also a human woman. I'm not powerless, and I won't stand by and watch my people suffer. I'll do whatever it takes to protect them, even if it means destroying you and your entire race." Her eyes narrowed. "So, I suggest you think carefully before you threaten me or anyone else."

The troll stared at her, his eyes widening in surprise before he finally nodded. "Very well, human. You have made your point."

Rianna smiled. "Good. Now, let's get back to the topic at hand. We need to figure out a way to distribute the resources fairly and make sure everyone has what they need."

Halox nodded. "Yes, and we also need to establish trade between the realms, to exchange goods and services to ensure we all thrive in this new environment."

The trolls and other leaders grumbled, but they eventually agreed to the terms. She was relieved they had come to an accord, but the real challenge was keeping them to the terms.

She whispered to Halox, "What will happen if one of them breaks the agreement?"

He frowned. "Then we'll have no choice but to punish them. We can't allow disobedience to go unpunished. That will only lead to chaos."

She sighed. "In the meantime, I think we should try to get the Mythic leaders to meet with the human leaders. A treaty holds more weight if more people sign on, right?"

He looked thoughtful. "That's a good idea, love. We can arrange a meeting and see if we can convince them to join the alliance."

She smiled, hopeful they could convince the humans to work with them. The Mythics might be powerful, but they weren't invincible. They needed the humans to want to be their mates, except for those who would steal an Omega. They didn't care about cooperation, but with enough pressure, they'd be forced to conform or leave Earth.

"I think it's important for the humans to see that you're not all monsters. You're just trying to survive, like they are. They need to understand you're not the enemy, even if you're not human."

Halox's eyes softened, and he leaned down to press a kiss to her forehead. "You're a wise female, love. I'm lucky to have you as my mate."

She blushed, her heart fluttering at his praise. "I'm lucky to have you too."

He smiled, his gaze full of affection. "Come. Let's discuss how we can talk to the human leaders and see if they're willing to meet with us."

She nodded and followed him, hoping they could convince the humans to give them a chance.

Chapter Ten—Halox

He started by speaking to the leader of New York City, though the mayor cowered in his office and refused to see him. Halox barreled through the doorway, bending the frame, and stood over the man as Rianna followed at a more sedate pace. It was strange to have her at his side when he'd handled all negotiations—or more truthfully, confrontations—by himself in the past, but she was wise, and he hoped having her along would make humans more receptive to hearing him.

"I'm told you're the leader of this city," he said in a low rumble.

"Y-yes," the human stammered. "I'm Mayor Andrew Monarky."

"I am Halox, Supreme General of the orc army. I have a proposition for you."

The human swallowed hard. "A p-proposition?"

"Yes. My people and I have been discussing how to ensure the safety of all races, and we've decided to create an alliance. We would like you to join us."

Mayor Monarky blinked. "An alliance? With the orcs?"

Halox nodded. "Yes. An alliance with the orcs, the centaurs, and other Mythic races."

The human looked skeptical. "Why would you want to form an alliance with us?"

"Because we need to work together to ensure the survival of everyone. There are limited resources, and we need to share them. We need to help each other, or we'll all perish." He made his tone firmer. "We're here for mates, and we will have them, but we want the relationships to be mutually beneficial and desirable to the Omegas with whom the magic matches us. We can't do that if your people are starving and dying."

"I...I see." The mayor's expression was still wary, but Halox saw a glimmer of hope in his eyes.

"We're willing to bring supplies from our realms to help feed your people in exchange for your cooperation and allowing us to stay and woo our human mates. We're also willing to provide protection and resources to help rebuild your cities and infrastructure."

Monarky's eyes widened. "You're offering to help us?"

Halox nodded. "Yes, but we need your cooperation. We need you to agree to the terms of the alliance and work with us to ensure the safety and prosperity of all races."

The human hesitated, then nodded. "All right. What do you want me to do?"

Rianna stepped forward then. "You have a lot of clout, Mr. Monarky. We'd like you to contact other human leaders and arrange a summit at the UN building in a few weeks. Call as many world leaders to get involved as you can."

He hesitated before nodding slowly. "I can try, but you must know, miss, that most humans view the monsters...Mythics as invaders and the enemy. It won't be easy to convince them to work with you."

Rianna sighed. "I know, but we have to try. This is the only way we can ensure the survival of all races."

Monarky nodded again, more firmly this time. "I'll do my best."

Halox clapped him on the back, making the human stagger. "Good. We'll be in touch."

They left the office, and Halox turned to Rianna. "I hope this works, love."

She smiled. "It will. I have faith in the humans."

He pulled her into his arms, pressing a kiss to her lips. "I have faith in you, my mate."

She laughed and kissed him back.

The next few weeks were busy as they prepared for the summit. Halox worked hard to ensure the orcs had enough supplies to bring from their realm, while Rianna coordinated with the other races to make sure they were ready as well.

The day of the summit arrived, and Halox was nervous. He didn't show it, of course, but the fate of his people—and this world—rested on the success of this meeting. He was stunned to arrive at the UN building with Rianna and find thousands of humans crowding around the outside, holding signs and shouting for the Mythics to leave.

He had expected resistance, but not quite so much. His mate took his hand and squeezed it reassuringly. "They'll come around, Halox. Just give them time."

He nodded, but he wasn't so sure. Still, he had to believe the humans would eventually see they were the key to the survival of all races. If they didn't, it would mean the end of everything.

The security guards allowed them to enter the building, though they eyed the orcs warily. Halox couldn't blame them. His warriors looked intimidating, but they wouldn't harm anyone unless provoked.

The atmosphere inside was tense. The various leaders and

representatives of the different countries and regions sat in their respective seats, eyeing each other and the Mythics with suspicion and distrust. Rianna led Halox to the front of the room, where she introduced him to the other leaders.

She spoke confidently, her voice carrying throughout the chamber. "I know this is difficult for all of you, but I promise the orcs and other Mythics don't want to hurt you. They're just looking for mates, and they're willing to share their resources to help us all survive. We need to work together, or we'll all die."

The leaders murmured amongst themselves, but Rianna's words seemed to resonate with some of them. Halox spoke then, his deep voice echoing through the room. "We're not here to conquer you. We're here to find mates and build a life for ourselves. We're willing to share our resources and help you rebuild your world, but we need your cooperation."

Some of the leaders were still skeptical, but others seemed more open to the idea. Halox knew it would take time for them to trust the Mythics, but he was determined to prove that they were worthy allies.

Rianna smiled at him, and his heart swelled with pride and admiration for his mate. She was formidable, and he was honored to have her by his side.

The summit continued for several hours, with both sides presenting their arguments and negotiating the terms of the alliance. Finally, it seemed like they were ready to vote on the idea of an alliance. Halox believed some countries would refuse, including Norway and Japan. Nothing he said could convince them. He maintained hope enough would be in favor to make it work.

A rumbling sound filled the air, and the ground shook beneath their feet. Rianna grabbed his arm, her eyes wide with fear. "Halox, what's happening?"

He frowned. "I don't know."

The shaking grew more violent, and the roof began to crack

and crumble as chunks of debris fell to the floor. The humans screamed in terror. "We have to get out of here," he shouted. "The building is collapsing."

He scooped Rianna into his arms and raced for the exit, dodging falling debris and panicked humans. They burst out of the doors into the street, and he set down his mate. All around them, buildings were collapsing, and people were running and screaming.

Halox looked up and saw the sky was dark with smoke and dust. He looked at Rianna, who was pale with fear. "What's happening?"

She shook her head, her eyes wide with shock. "I don't know, but it looks like a bomb went off."

Halox's blood ran cold. "A bomb? Who would do such a thing?"

Rianna's face was grim. "I don't know, but they clearly want to destroy us all."

The crowd of protesters was scattering around them, but his gaze fixed on several with their protest signs. "It was the humans. They did this."

She frowned. "You can't be sure of that."

He pointed to the group of protesters, who were fleeing in the opposite direction. "They're the ones who were here to protest. They're the ones who are trying to kill us."

Rianna's eyes widened, and she looked at the fleeing humans. "That's a big leap, Halox. Protesting is an intrinsic part of the democratic process, especially in America. You're just assuming it was them."

"It seems evident, Lady Rianna," said Taxlos in his rumbling voice. "Crowds are often violent. The humans are afraid of us, and they're lashing out."

Rianna shook her head. "No, that doesn't make sense. Why would they destroy their own city and leaders? They're not stupid. They know they need to work together with us if they want to survive."

He pitied his mate. "You can't see the duplicity of your kind, but I do." He turned to Taxlos. "Gather as many as you can for interrogation."

"Yes, General. As you command."

Rianna's eyes widened. "Wait, what are you doing?"

"I'm going to find out who's responsible for this attack, and I'm going to punish them."

He strode off, leaving Rianna staring after him. He knew she didn't understand, but he couldn't let this attack go unanswered. The humans had made their position clear, and now it was time for the orcs to retaliate.

A group of human delegates exited the UN, looking frightened as they warily approached him. "What's happening? Is it safe to leave?"

Halox growled. "The human protestors attacked us. They bombed the UN building, and they're trying to kill us all."

The humans looked shocked and horrified. "That's impossible." The mayor shook his head. "Why would our people do this?"

"They disapproved of the idea of an alliance and are willing to kill to prevent it." He looked at the mayor. "See to your wounded and dead while we investigate which humans did this."

A premier from a country whose name he'd forgotten straightened her shoulders. "I don't trust you to investigate without bias, Mr. Halox."

"General." He bared his teeth. "General Halox The Bloody of Clan Falcox, and I will have vengeance. I don't care what you think."

The woman's eyes flashed with anger. "This is my planet, and I'll not let you take it over."

"You're welcome to it." He gestured at the destruction. "If you can live in this, by all means, take it. Otherwise, you'll need to accept our aid and work with us."

She maintained a firm expression. "Allowing you to

instantly assume humans did this without adequate investigation isn't working together. We shall conduct our own investigations and focus on the more likely source—the Mythics."

"You dare accuse us?"

"I dare. You've already proven you're willing to attack humans."

"After humans started a violent clash with my people and the other Mythics."

"You can't prove that," said the French delegate.

"And you can't prove it was us." Halox glared at the humans. "We were in the middle of a peaceful negotiation, and you attacked us. I will find the culprits, and I'll make them pay."

The humans looked at each other, and he could see the fear and uncertainty in their eyes. They were scared, and they didn't know what to do.

Rianna came up to him and put a hand on his arm. "Halox, please. Let's not jump to conclusions. We need to investigate this and find out who's really responsible."

He looked at her, his heart aching at the sight of her beautiful face streaked with dirt and ash. "I know it was the humans, Rianna. I can feel it in my bones."

She shook her head. "I don't believe that. I think some group of Mythics is behind this, and they're trying to frame the humans."

"Why would we do such a thing? We need the humans to survive."

She frowned. "You don't need all the humans. Your kind only needs the Omegas. Can you really pretend there aren't those among the Mythics who would happily get rid of the other humans who serve no purpose in their minds? I'm sure there are plenty who think they could take over the realm without any trouble."

Halox wanted to deny it, but he couldn't. There were

certainly Mythics who would be happy to see all but the Omegas of the human race wiped out.

Rianna sighed. "We need to work together, Halox. We need to find out who's responsible for this attack, and we need to make sure it never happens again." Her hand squeezed his arm. "Please don't react in anger and pursue humans indiscriminately. I'm asking you to do a proper investigation in cooperation with the humans."

Her eyes were pleading, and he couldn't deny her. He nodded. "Very well, love. I'll do as you ask. We'll investigate and find the true culprits."

Rianna smiled, and his heart swelled with pride that she was willing to stand up to him even when he was angry and determined to exact revenge. "Come. You need rest." He turned to the humans. "We'll coordinate our investigative efforts." His words were stiff, and he still didn't trust them, but they were right. He lacked enough proof as of now to be sure it was the protestors.

They returned to the orc encampment, and Halox settled Rianna into their tent. She was exhausted and fell asleep almost immediately, but he remained awake, thinking about the events of the day.

He was angry and frustrated that the humans would resort to such violence, but he also understood their fear. They were desperate to survive, and they would do whatever it took to protect their people. Still, he couldn't let this go unpunished. They would find the perpetrators and bring them to justice. He wouldn't let the humans get away with this attack or destroy the fragile peace between the races.

He was brooding about it when Taxlos came to him, grunting a greeting and swishing the tent flap. He slipped out to join his second.

"We captured thirty humans. They were just…lying there. It was quite strange. They're all being held in cages at the zoo."

His first reaction was satisfaction quickly followed by unease. He'd promised Rianna to conduct a fair investigation with the humans. Yet these were witnesses. It was senseless to release them without interrogation. "I'll speak to them."

Taxlos nodded. "As you wish, General."

Halox made his way to the zoo, which was located on the edge of Central Park. Right now, it was still unclaimed, and the other races had allowed the zookeepers to tend to the animals, not wanting wild animals running through the city and causing more chaos.

He entered the zoo and made his way to the primate exhibit after Taxlos directed him there to speak with the humans running the facility. Inside, he found a group of humans huddled together, looking terrified.

"I'm General Halox, in charge of the orc army."

One of the humans, a woman, stepped forward. "I'm Dr. Maddy Lassiter, the director of the zoo. We're just trying to take care of the animals. We had nothing to do with the bombing."

Halox studied her, noting her defiant expression. "I understand that. We're merely using this facility to hold some prisoners until questioning is over. Once we've determined they're innocent, they'll be released."

"And if they're guilty?" Her voice was soft, but he heard the challenge in her tone.

"They'll be punished."

"How?"

"That depends on the crime. We orcs are known for our brutality, but we're not cruel. We'll give them a fair trial and determine a fitting punishment."

Maddy nodded, seeming to accept his answer. "What do you want from us?"

Halox sighed. "I just need you to stay out of our way. We'll be conducting our investigation, and we don't need any interference."

"I understand."

Halox nodded and turned to leave, but Maddy's voice stopped him.

"I just want you to know, we support the idea of an alliance. There's no going back to the way things were, and we need to find a way to move forward. We need your help, and we're willing to work with you."

Halox turned back to her, surprised by her words. "You are?"

She nodded. "Yes. I know not all humans feel the same way, but I believe we can make this work. We can't keep fighting each other. It will only lead to more death and destruction."

Halox considered her words. "I agree. We need to work together if we're going to survive." He paused. "I'll be in touch. Stay out of our way, and we'll stay out of yours."

Maddy nodded. "Deal."

Halox left the exhibit, following Taxlos to a group of cages that appeared to have been unused before repurposing to a hasty jail. The humans inside looked scared and confused, and Halox felt a twinge of sympathy for them.

"We need to question them," said Halox to his second. "We need to find out if any of them had anything to do with the bombing."

"Yes, General."

Halox watched as the orcs began to question the humans. Most denied having anything to do with the attack, but all were proud to have been protesting the proposed alliance.

"You're monsters. You don't belong here," shouted one man.

Halox glared at him. "We belong here as much as you do. We're here for mates, and we're willing to share our resources to help you survive."

"We wouldn't need them if you hadn't come to our world," said a human female.

Taxlos smirked. "You were doing such a good job being stewards of this planet and managing your resources, were you?"

She flushed and looked away.

"We're not here to destroy you. We're here to help you. We have the resources and strength to rebuild your cities and restore order. We can help you thrive again."

The humans looked at each other, but none of them spoke.

"We're not the monsters here," said Halox. "You are. You're the ones who bombed a building full of innocent people."

"We didn't," said the man who'd yelled at him to leave. He sounded more reasonable now. "We were standing there when a sort of…blackness descended."

"It was so cold," said a young woman as she hugged herself, shivering. "And then there was a bright light, and I passed out."

Halox stared at them. "You didn't see anything else?"

The humans shook their heads.

"I think they're telling the truth, General," said Taxlos. "They're just as clueless as we are." He turned to the woman with whom he'd verbally sparred about the planet. "You. Tell me how you felt when the blackness descended."

"Fear. I was scared, and I thought I was going to die." She shivered. "My mind was filled with dark images. I couldn't see much, but I heard and felt shouts and screams…blood dripping on me… I don't ever want to feel that way again."

The orcs exchanged a glance. "Do you think it was magic? Something to scare you and make you feel that way?"

She shrugged. "I don't know. I'm not a witch or a mage. I don't know much about magic or human weapons. I just know what I experienced."

Halox nodded. "Very well. You may go."

"Just like that?" she asked, sounding incredulous. "You're letting us go?"

"Yes. You're free to go."

"But what about the others?"

"We'll continue to question them," said Taxlos. "We need to find out who was responsible for the attack, and we won't stop until we do."

She squared her shoulders. "I'm not leaving without all the humans I came with."

Taxlos growled low in his throat. "Very well, human female. You will stay with me while we conduct the questioning of the other cages." He looked at the humans behind the woman. "You're all free to go."

Unlike the female with her strange green cat-like eyes and blonde hair, they didn't hesitate to scatter and flee.

Halox observed Taxlos's eyes widening and heard the purr emanating from his chest as he turned from his second and the woman. He recognized the signs. The Alpha had found his intended Omega.

"I won't let you hurt them," she said behind Halox.

"You couldn't stop me, female." Yet his voice was surprisingly tender. "What's your name?"

She hesitated for a long moment. "Erin Morney."

"I am Taxlos, Erin Morney. I will not harm you or the others. I'm an honorable orc, and I will keep you safe." He lowered his voice, though Halox still heard him. "I will protect you, my Omega."

She gasped, making Halox turn to observe them since she sounded so fearful. Not that Taxlos would hurt her, but he was poised to assure her of that. "What did you call me?"

"You're my Omega, love. I will protect you and provide for you." His eyes roamed over her body, lingering on her breasts and hips. "And I'll give you many strong young."

She blushed, but Halox saw the interest in her eyes. "I'm not an Omega. I'm a human woman."

"You will be mine, and you'll bear my children."

She stared at him, her eyes wide and her cheeks flushed. "I...I don't know what to say."

"Say you'll be mine, love."

"I..."

He cleared his throat. "Sorry to interrupt, but we must speak to the other humans."

Taxlos seemed to regain control of himself and fell into step with Halox when he resumed walking, keeping Erin on his other side. "Of course, General."

The next cage contained the humans the orcs had been unable to locate earlier. They all claimed to have been at the protest, but their stories were all similar to the humans in the first cage.

"I don't know how we got here," said one man. "I remember being at the protest, and then everything went black. When I woke up, I was in a cage."

"I think someone used magic to transport us here," said another. "I've heard rumors there are witches and mages among the Mythics."

"There are magic users among the humans now too." Halox sighed. "This feels more mystical than technological. I believe you all. Taxlos, open the cage." When his second had done so, he said, "Go home."

The humans wasted no time in escaping, and Halox didn't blame them. They had no idea if the Mythics would be lenient, and they didn't want to stick around to find out. He was about to return to Fort Tyron when Taxlos roared behind him.

He whirled around, looking for the source of attack. "What?"

"My mate. She ran in the chaos of the others escaping."

Halox winced with sympathy as he clapped his friend on his broad shoulder. "I know the pain of the chase well, my friend, but when you catch her..." He sighed in contentment as he recalled Rianna's sweet submission after their binding ceremony. "You'll have the best sex of your life."

"I'm not *chasing* her. I'm going to find her and bring her to my tent."

Halox hid a smile. "You have my permission to take a week of leave."

"Thank you, General."

Halox left his friend to his hunt and headed back to his own tent, where Rianna was waiting for him. He should tell her about the humans they'd interrogated, but he held off as she rolled over sleepily and gave him a smile despite their earlier words of disagreement.

"Where were you?" she asked as she opened her arms to him.

He crawled onto the bed and gathered her into his embrace. After a hesitation, he said, "I was checking on the humans we captured."

Rianna stiffened. "What humans? Who did you capture? You said you'd work with the human authorities to investigate."

"I did, but I'd already instructed Taxlos to gather them before that agreement. You must remember because you were there."

She nodded after a moment, still looking disgruntled. "Okay, but keeping them violates the spirit of the agreement."

"They're not being held anymore. I questioned and released them."

She relaxed against him. "Oh, okay."

"I don't think they were involved in the bombing. They all claim they were at the protest, and then some type of darkness descended on them, and they saw and felt horrible things before passing out. Taxlos and my warriors gathered them while they were out and put them in the cages, but they don't remember that part. They only remember waking up in the cages."

Rianna frowned. "That's strange. It sounds like the effects

of a spell or something."

"That's what I thought too. I think someone used magic to make us think the humans were responsible for a bombing, but it was a magical attack instead.

Rianna's eyes widened. "That's...that's terrible. Who would do such a thing? And why?"

"I don't know, but I intend to find out." He cleared his throat. "You've probably realized not all Mythics are allies. There are some enemies among us who have fought each other for centuries. The prospect of finding mates might allow them to work together, or it might drive them to greater conflict."

Rianna bit her lip. "I'm worried this will all fall apart. The humans didn't even commit to the alliance before the attack."

He pulled her close, kissing her forehead. "Don't worry, love. We'll find the culprits, and we'll fix this."

Rianna nodded, but he could see the doubt and fear in her eyes.

"Trust me, Rianna. I won't let anyone hurt you."

"I know you'll protect me, but I'm worried about everyone else. What if they start attacking each other? What if there's another war?" She buried her face in his chest. "I don't want to lose you."

"You won't. I promise." He kissed her softly. "Now, get some rest. We'll figure this out tomorrow."

Rianna nodded and snuggled closer to him, her body warm and soft against his. In a short time, she dozed off, her gentle snores filling the tent.

He laid awake, his mind racing with possibilities. He needed to find the culprits and punish them, but he also needed to ensure the safety of his people and the humans. It was a daunting task, but he was determined to succeed. There was no other option.

CHAPTER ELEVEN—RIANNA

Rianna awoke to the sound of Halox's deep breathing. She was encouraged that he'd let the humans go last night, but she wasn't entirely sure he could remain unbiased. She carefully eased out from under his heavy arm and dressed, slipping out of the tent, and leaving the fort quickly. She moved with purpose so no one would dare stop and ask what she was doing.

She walked to the park, where she found the mayor and several of the other leaders who'd attended the summit. They were huddled together, talking in hushed tones.

"Mayor Monarky," she called out.

He turned to her, his face pale and drawn. "Dr. Goodwin. What are you doing here?"

"I wanted to check on you and see how you're doing."

He shook his head. "It's bad, Doctor. So many people were killed in the blast. We don't have the resources to deal with the aftermath and the injured."

Rianna's heart ached for them. "I'm so sorry, Mayor. I wish

there was more I could do to help." She hesitated. "We have healers, and they have magical medicine. I'll ask some to volunteer. Where did you move the survivors? The UN is a pile of rubble."

"The convention center."

She nodded. "I'll have the orcs bring supplies and the healers."

"Thank you, Dr. Goodwin. That would be very helpful." He frowned at her. "Why are you here alone?"

He clearly expected Halox to be with her at all times. Since her mate basically expected the same, she couldn't fault the mayor's assumption. She gave him a small smile. "Some witnesses indicated it might have been a magical attack, so I came to see if I could detect lingering magic."

"That's why you sneaked out alone?" asked Halox in a surprisingly mild tone behind her.

She jumped and spun around to face him. "I didn't sneak out. I just wanted to come and see if I could help."

Halox's expression softened. "I understand, love, but you should have told me, and you should have brought Lirra. She's your guard. I assigned her to you."

Rianna sighed. "I know, but I didn't want to wake your sister. Besides, I can take care of myself." She smiled. "You saw what I did to the centaurs."

Halox raised an eyebrow. "You're an Omega, Rianna. A powerful one, but still an Omega. You're not invincible." He drew her away from the humans. "Some Alphas won't care that you bear my scent mark, or that you aren't their fated mate. They'll take what they want anyway, because you can physically accommodate them. You would be injured, and you would probably lose the babe."

Rianna's eyes widened with horror. "That would kill me."

"It would kill me too, once I killed them." He held her closer. "Please don't misunderstand. Very few Alphas are like that, but there are some who are vicious predators."

"Like some humans." She nodded slowly. "I understand and promise to be more careful."

He smiled. "Good. Now, let's see if we can find any traces of magic."

They searched the area, and she detected faint traces of dark magic. "It's definitely magic, Halox, but I can't identify the signature. It's not familiar to me."

He frowned. "I don't recognize it either. It's not the centaurs' magic, nor is it the trolls' energy. It feels old...ancient... Somehow familiar, but not."

Rianna shuddered. "It's creepy. It makes me feel like I'm being hunted."

"I feel that too." He wrapped his arm around her. "Let's go back to the fort. I don't want to risk you being out here with the magic lingering."

She hesitated. "Actually..."

He paused. "Yes?"

"I need to do something. Alone."

His eyes narrowed. "Didn't you hear my warning about other Alphas, not to mention those who might target you for being my mate? There is resentment against you on both sides."

There'd be even more humans resenting her if they learned she'd opened the portal. "I heard and understand, but there's someone who knows a lot more about magic than I do. She won't appreciate it if I bring you along to ask if she recognizes the signature of this magic."

"Who is this person?"

Rianna sighed. "She's a witch. Her name is Aislinn. You met her briefly when you found me hiding in her home when you were still chasing me."

He snorted. "The distraction spell. I remember."

"Yes. She's the Keeper."

His eyes widened. "The Keeper? What's that?"

Should she tell him? After a moment of wrestling with

herself, deciding she didn't want to keep more secrets between them, she said, "None of the Mythics know why the portal closed."

He shook his head. "No. Our histories have always said it was a dark magic."

"It wasn't dark, but it was magic—fed by the combined magic of the witches of Earth."

He stared at her. "What?" He huffed. "Why would they do that?"

"Because they were afraid of you. You're big and strong, and you can fight. Your kind is violent, and you're not afraid to use your strength and power. The women of this planet were weak and defenseless in comparison, and they didn't want to be conquered. They were tired of being ruled by men who were bigger and stronger than them. They didn't want to be raped and beaten and treated as less than human or forced to become Omegas."

He looked stunned. "We never meant to conquer them. We were just looking for mates. We would have protected them and provided for them. They would have been revered and loved."

She searched for a delicate way to phrase it. "That might be your intentions now, but Alphas of the past were a lot more brutal. They virtually enslaved their Omegas, ruling over and controlling them. The Omegas rebelled, and Aislinn's coven coordinated the spell to seal the portal and keep it sealed."

Looking down, she confessed the last big secret. "She asked me not to do the supercollider experiment, fearing it might rip open the portal due to the waning magic in our world and difficulty keeping it closed. I didn't listen. If I hadn't conducted the experiment with the black hole, your kind would still be locked out of Earth. I'm responsible for all of this."

Halox sighed. "I'm glad you did it, Rianna. I wouldn't have found you otherwise." He paused. "You're not responsible for the actions of your ancestors, love. They made the decision to cast the spell, not you. Perhaps my ancestors gave them good reason to want to expel them." He looked uncomfortable with the thought. "I can't believe all my kind were like that. We have our share of brutes, but most of us are honorable." He shook his head. "You have to stop blaming yourself for what happened. The past is the past. We need to focus on the future."

She nodded. "You're right, but I still have very mixed emotions about what I did." She cleared her throat. "You can see why Aislinn won't speak to me or answer my summoning spell if you're with me?"

"She fears I'll retaliate for what her coven did to my kind?"

"Yes. She doesn't trust you."

He sighed. "I can't say I blame her. I don't trust most humans." He looked at her. "You're the exception. You're the only human I truly trust."

She coughed to clear the sudden lump in her throat. "I love you, Halox."

"I love you too, Rianna." He cupped her cheek. "I agree to leave the area so you can summon Aislinn, but not until Lirra is here to protect you."

She bit her lip but nodded. "I think Aislinn will accept her presence."

"Good." Halox summoned his sister via a spell, and the warrior arrived within minutes, looking annoyed.

"What is it, brother?"

"I need you to watch over my mate while she summons a witch."

Lirra frowned. "A witch? Why?"

Halox explained about the dark magic, and Lirra nodded. "Very well. I'll keep Rianna safe."

He kissed Rianna. "Be careful, love. I'll be nearby, waiting for you."

She nodded. "I will."

He left the area, and she began to draw the circle and cast the spell to summon Aislinn. As she finished, the air shimmered, and the witch appeared. Her red hair was wild, and her blue eyes flashed with anger. She looked rough, like she'd been living a hard life in the past few months.

It filled Rianna with renewed remorse for how her actions had changed everyone's lives, though she was glad it had brought her Halox. "Hello, Aislinn. Thank you for answering my spell."

"What do you want, Rianna? I'm busy."

"I need your help. You've heard about the attack here yesterday?" At the witch's nod, she said, "There's some sort of dark magic in the area, and I need to know if you recognize it."

Aislinn frowned. "Dark magic?"

"Yes. It's ancient and powerful, and it feels like it's hunting." She shivered. "It's terrifying."

"I'll do a divination." She pulled a pouch from her cloak and sprinkled herbs on the ground. She lit them with a wave of her hand, and they burned with a purple flame.

"What are you doing?" asked Lirra with genuine curiosity.

"I'm performing a divination to find the source of the magic. It's a spell to reveal the truth." Aislinn looked at Rianna. "Show me the location where you felt the magic."

She led the way to the spot, and Aislinn closed her eyes, chanting softly. The flames flared, and the smoke swirled into a spiral. The air grew cold, and Rianna shivered.

"The magic is coming from the north," said Aislinn.

Rianna frowned. "That's odd. The Mythics are all concentrated in the south."

"Not all of them," said Aislinn. "There are some who have migrated to the mountains and the forests, far away from civilization, and they're not friendly to humans."

"What are they?"

"Mostly ogres, trolls, and giants. They're not interested in mating with humans or sharing this world with them. Their own realms are in tatters, and they're here ostensibly for survival, but I'm sure their ultimate goal is supremacy and annihilation of those they deem inferior." Her expression turned grim. "They're the ones you need to worry about, who will do anything to stop this alliance."

"Why?" asked Lirra. "The Mythics I know want love and families."

Aislinn looked unsettled by that but didn't argue. "This magic is old. Far older than anything I know. I need to consult with my coven, but someone must be leading the faction that did this attack."

Rianna was shaky but moderately relieved. "So, it wasn't the Mythics in this area or the humans?"

"No. This was an outside force, and it's not the first time we've felt it." The witch looked uneasy. "We've been sensing it since the beginning of closing the portal, but there was a...membrane, I guess you could say. It was a different kind of barrier on the portal when Mythics were here before, designed to keep out certain creatures. This power continues to probe and tries to break through periodically ever since we closed the portal. As magic faded on Earth, it became stronger, and my coven genuinely feared we couldn't withstand its next attempt."

"Then I opened the portal."

"Yes."

"I'm sorry."

"I'm not. I'm grateful for the additional magic, and the fact that the Mythics are here now means we'll be able to defeat whatever is trying to break through, or at least recreate the barrier that filtered out the source of this magical signature." Aislinn was clearly troubled by the realization she was glad the Mythics had returned. "I've always regarded them...you," She glanced at Lirra, "All as the enemy, but now, our combined efforts might be all that stops whatever this is. I don't like it, but I'll accept it."

"Thank you." Lirra inclined her head.

"Don't thank me yet. We have a long way to go before we can stop this." She looked at Rianna. "I'll consult with my coven and try to determine the source of this magic. In the meantime, you need to be careful. There are forces at work here that are beyond our comprehension."

Rianna nodded. "I'll be careful, and I'll keep an eye out for anything unusual."

"Good." Aislinn vanished in a swirl of smoke.

Rianna turned to Lirra. "Halox should return so we can tell the humans." They were still gathered, whispering and processing the attack scene with a crime scene unit, though she knew that wouldn't tell them anything.

"I'll fetch him."

She returned with Halox, and the two of them approached the mayor. "Mayor Monarky."

He turned to them. "Yes?"

"We believe we know what caused the explosion," said Halox.

The mayor's eyes widened. "What was it?"

"Magic," said Rianna. "Old, dark magic. We believe it was used to make us think the humans were responsible for the attack and to make you think the Mythics were responsible."

The mayor frowned. "I see. Do you have any idea who's behind it?"

She shook her head. "No, but we'll keep investigating and let you know as soon as we find anything."

"Thank you, Dr. Goodwin. We appreciate your help." He looked at Halox. "And yours as well, General."

Halox nodded. "We're all in this together, Mayor."

The mayor nodded. "Agreed." He cleared his throat. "Once we have answers, we'll attempt to reconvene to share them and vote on the alliance."

"Very well. We'll continue to investigate and share information as we have it."

The mayor nodded and walked away, and Rianna watched him go. "I hope we can convince the humans to ally with the Mythics. We need each other." She shivered as a lingering trace of dark magic washed over her again. "Something terrible is coming, and we need to be prepared."

Halox wrapped his arm around her shoulders. "We will be. We'll find the culprits and make them pay."

Rianna hoped he was right but expected it to be much harder than he made it sound.

The orcs continued their investigation, and she worked with the human authorities to help them identify and locate the victims of the bombing while a surprising number of orc healers and other Mythics volunteered to help with the human survivors at the makeshift hospital in the convention center. There had been no casualties on the Mythics' side, so they were able to focus on helping the human survivors recover.

It was a long week of seemingly never-ending work when Halox virtually kidnapped her from the convention center, picking her up and striding with her into the trees of Central Park. "What are you doing?"

"Ensuring my mate relaxes." He set her down on a blanket spread on the grass and handed her a plate of food. "Eat."

She took the plate and obediently began to eat, realizing how hungry she was. She'd been working nonstop for days, and she'd barely eaten. She sighed in pleasure as she ate the orc delicacy. "This is delicious. What is it?"

"It's called *pulagago*—a type of bread stuffed with meat and vegetables."

She nodded and kept eating, enjoying the fresh air and sunshine. "How did you manage to get this?"

"I have my ways." He grinned. "I asked Taxlos' mother to prepare it."

"Where is Taxlos?"

"He's guarding the perimeter of the park. He has a team of warriors with him." He shook his head, still smiling. "His leave ended, but his mate continues to elude him."

"You sound amused."

He laughed. "Perhaps a little, though I know how frustrating it can be. I chased you for over a week, remember?"

She smiled. "I remember. I was terrified of you."

"I know, but I didn't want to hurt you."

"I know that now, but at the time, I was convinced you were a monster who wanted to rape me and impregnate me with your spawn."

He winced. "I'm sorry, love. I wish I could go back and change things."

"Me too." She sighed. "I hope Taxlos can win over his Omega."

"I'm sure he will. He's a determined male, and he's not giving up."

Rianna nodded. "I'm not surprised. Orcs are stubborn bastards." She grinned. "Present company included, of course."

Halox growled and nipped at her neck. "I'll show you stubborn, love."

"Ooh, I look forward to it."

He chuckled and kissed her. "I love you, Rianna."

"I love you too, Halox." She shoveled in the last bite of the *pulagago* as he pushed her onto her back, tugging at her pants.

He stilled when he had her stripped from the waist down, and her shirt pushed under her breasts. Halox cupped her abdomen, staring down with wonder. "You're showing, my mate."

She smiled. "I know. I figured you'd noticed. I'm starting to get a little round."

"You carry my child, and you're perfect." He leaned down

and kissed her stomach.

She stroked his hair, her heart swelling with love. "I'm so happy." Days spent toiling away for hours on end in her lab seemed almost like unpleasant memories now, though she'd once lived for such moments.

"I am too." He kissed her belly again before moving lower. The tone of his kisses changed, and he licked her pussy lips. "You taste so sweet, love."

Rianna moaned and squirmed as he teased her clit with his tongue. He lapped at her, making her writhe and moan beneath him.

"You like that, don't you?" he murmured.

"Yes."

"I want to hear you say it."

"I like it."

"Tell me what you want." He sucked her clit into his mouth, flicking his tongue over the sensitive bud.

"More."

"More what?"

"I want more. I want to orgasm."

He increased the pressure on her clit, and she gasped and arched her back. "Come for me, love."

She cried out as she came, her body shaking with the force of her release. Halox kissed her inner thighs, then moved up to her breasts, suckling her sensitive nipples.

"I want to fuck you, love," he whispered. "I want to fill your tight little cunt with my cock."

"Yes."

"You want that too, don't you?"

"Yes." She reached up and tugged at his armor. "Take this off."

He complied, stripping off his armor, trousers, and boots. His thick, heavy cock jutted out from his muscular body, and she licked her lips.

"Do you want to taste it?" he asked.

"Yes." She craved the salty, musky flavor of his pre-cum and the feel of his velvety skin on her tongue.

He knelt beside her head, and she eagerly took his massive shaft in her hands. She licked the tip, tasting his pre-cum. He groaned, and she smiled, taking him deeper. She bobbed her head, sucking him in and out of her mouth. He was so large around that she could only take in the head and an inch of his shaft. She used her hands to stroke the rest of his length, squeezing and stroking his cock as she sucked him.

He grunted and thrust his hips, shallowly fucking her mouth. "I wish the magic made your mouth able to accommodate me."

She pulled back and smiled. "You'd like that, wouldn't you? To be able to fuck my face and throat?"

He groaned. "Yes."

"I'd like that too." She took him in her hand and pumped him, watching his face contort with pleasure. "Would you like to be inside me now?"

"Yes." With a growl, he pulled away and flipped her onto her hands and knees. He was after total domination, so caught up in the moment, and she loved it.

He positioned himself behind her and thrust inside in one deep plunge, filling her completely. She moaned as he stretched her, her body adjusting to his size. He began to move, his pace slow and steady. She rocked back against him, meeting his thrusts.

"That's it, love. Squeeze my cock with your tight little cunt."

She tightened her muscles around him, and he groaned. "You feel so good, Halox. So big and hard inside me."

He gripped her hips and increased his pace, pounding into her. "I love being inside you, Rianna. You're perfect, love."

She whimpered as he hit a particularly sensitive spot deep inside her. "Right there." He angled his thrusts to hit that spot while grasping her hips. His fingers dug into her flesh, and she knew he would leave bruises, but she didn't care. She wanted him to mark her as his.

"You're mine, Rianna. Mine."

"Yes."

He pounded into her, his movements almost frenzied. "Tell me you're mine."

"I'm yours, Halox. Only yours."

He roared as he came, his seed flooding her channel as he continued to thrust. She followed him over the edge, her orgasm washing over her in waves. The intensity of it was overwhelming, and she collapsed onto the blanket, panting and gasping for breath.

Halox wrapped his arms around her and pulled her closer, kissing her shoulder as he remained covering her. She was still on her knees, but her face touched the blanket now. "Are you all right, love?"

She nodded. "I'm fine, Halox. That was amazing."

He smiled against her skin. "It was." With a sigh, he pulled out of her and rolled to his side, gathering her into his arms. "I love you, Rianna."

"I love you too, Halox." She snuggled close, content to stay there forever.

"I'm sorry I got carried away." He sounded sheepish. "I didn't mean to hurt you."

"It's okay." She flushed. "I liked it."

He chuckled. "So did I, but I'll try to be more gentle next time."

"There's nothing wrong with being a little rough now and then." She put a hand on her stomach. "Though we might have to take it easier for now. I don't want to risk hurting the baby."

"I agree. I want to protect you both." He kissed her forehead. "You're the most important thing in the world to me."

She smiled. "You're the most important thing to me too."

They laid there basking in the sun and each other's

presence. She closed her eyes, feeling at peace for the first time in weeks. She was safe and loved and Halox would always protect her, though she could take care of herself. She drifted off to sleep, secure in his embrace

CHAPTER TWELVE—RIANNA

When Aislinn sent a summoning spell a few days later, she had to answer it. First, she approached Halox, who was busy discussing something with Taxlos. "Halox, I need to go see Aislinn."

His eyes narrowed. "Why?"

"She summoned me. I think she's found out more about the magic."

Halox looked reluctant but nodded, clearly reluctant. "Please take Lirra."

"Of course." She kissed him before calling for Lirra and leading her back into the tent, where a small magical portal, quite different from the one she'd opened in the lab, hovered in the middle of the room. "Let's go."

Lirra nodded and stepped through the portal. Rianna followed her, emerging in another location she didn't completely recognize but thought might be Prospect Park. They were in a forest clearing, and Aislinn was waiting for them along with a dozen other witches.

"Welcome, Rianna." Aislinn smiled at Lirra. "Hello, warrior."

"Hello, witch."

Aislinn's smile widened. "I'm Aislinn."

"I'm Lirra."

"I'm pleased to properly meet you, Lirra."

"Likewise."

Aislinn turned to the others. "These are the members of my coven. We've been researching the magic, and we believe we've identified the source."

Rianna swallowed hard. "What is it?"

"It's the same magic that's been trying to break through the barrier for millennia. It's old and powerful, but it's not alone. There are other forces at work."

"What kind of forces?" asked Lirra.

"There's a group of beings who want to come through the portal and conquer Earth. They're not Mythics, and they're not human. They're something else entirely, and they're very dangerous."

"What are they?" asked Rianna.

"We don't know, but we believe they're linked to the dark magic signature or working with the spellcaster. They're the ones who have been trying to break through the barrier and who orchestrated the attack on the summit." She turned to a raven-haired witch beside her. "Do you have the drawing, Abby?"

Abby nodded and held up a piece of parchment. "I drew it from a spell that tapped into the dark energy signature." She passed it to Aislinn, who handed it to Rianna.

She looked down at the black nightmare on the page. The creature looked like a cross between a dragon and a demon. Its face was twisted and ugly, and its eyes glowed red with hatred. It had sharp teeth and claws, and its wings were leathery and batlike. The beast was covered in scales and spikes, and its edges looked smudged. "Was that deliberate?" She pointed to the overall shifting, blurry look of the thing.

"Yes. It's difficult to capture the image. The magic doesn't want us to see it." Abby shivered. "I think it might have the ability to at least partially shift its appearance or maybe move through and around barriers."

Rianna shuddered. "It's horrible. What is it?"

An old woman stepped forward. Her bearing was straight, and her pure white hair was in a neat bun. She looked ageless in some way, yet older than any human should look in another. "It's a nemataur."

"This is Eleanor, my great-grandmother. She was the Keeper before me," said Aislinn.

Rianna nodded respectfully. "It's a pleasure to meet you, ma'am."

Eleanor smiled. "Likewise, Dr. Goodwin."

"Please, call me Rianna."

"Rianna." Eleanor's expression turned grave. "The nemataurs are ancient creatures of evil. They were created by the fae to battle their enemies, the kattarin, but they were inherently uncontrollable and turned against the fae, aligning with the kattarin. The Mythics banished them to another dimension, but they're trying to find a way back here."

"Why do they want to conquer Earth?" asked Lirra.

"They want to destroy all life and turn this realm into a barren wasteland. They were designed by ancient fae magic to feed on death and destruction."

Rianna felt sick. "That's terrible."

"They have a weakness. Sunlight," said Eleanor. "Unfortunately, they also have an ally in Theron."

Rianna frowned. "Who's Theron?"

"He's a Mythic who's been secretly working with the nemataur for years. He wants to rule the Mythics, and he'll do whatever it takes to achieve that goal."

"What does he want with the humans?" asked Rianna.

"He's using them as a distraction. He's hoping to pit the

Mythics and the humans against each other so he can swoop in and take control when the dust settles." Eleanor looked troubled. "He probably wants Omegas too, for he is a Mythic, but he won't be interested in consenting mates."

Rianna's blood ran cold. "What will he do to them?"

"He'll use them as breeding stock, and he won't be gentle. He'll want to breed them as quickly as possible, and he'll use magic to ensure they become pregnant." She paused. "He's a kattarin, and his kind is nearly extinct following the Fae Wars. He'll want a harem of Omegas to replenish his race while he destroys the other Mythics. He's a ruthless bastard."

Rianna felt faint. "Why would he work with nemataurs if they drain the life from everything?"

"The original alliance with nemataurs and kattarin was probably an 'enemy of my enemy' situation," said Aislinn. "With Theron, we believe he plans to take what he wants from this planet, including Omegas, and then pick one of the other Mythic realms to inhabit, leaving the nemataurs to consume everything else they can reach via the Earth portal."

"How do you know all that?" asked Lirra.

"We've been communicating with a group of banshees since the portal closed. They're one of the few who can resist the nemataurs' magic and Theron's influence, and they've been keeping tabs on the situation."

Rianna frowned. "I thought you hated all Mythics?"

"We do, but banshees are different. They're not like the other Mythics. They don't want to conquer or enslave humans, and they're not interested in Omegas." Aislinn looked uncomfortable. "They're asexual."

Rianna's eyes widened. "Really?"

"Yes. They reproduce by budding, and they're very long-lived. They'll outlive us all."

"That's fascinating," said Rianna.

Lirra looked skeptical. "Now's not the time for a lesson on the banshee life cycle. No offense. If they're immune to the nemataurs, why haven't they stopped them?"

Aislinn sighed. "They're not strong enough to defeat them. They've been evading them for centuries, but the nemataurs are powerful. The banshees don't have sufficient numbers or enough power to take on a horde of nemataurs."

"So, what do we do?" asked Rianna.

"We need to join forces with the Mythics and the humans if we're going to stand a chance of defeating them." Eleanor lifted her chin. "It's the only way."

Rianna nodded slowly. "I'll speak to Halox and the humans. We're trying to form an alliance, but the attack on the summit set us back."

"We'll do the same," said Aislinn. "We have to stop the nemataurs before they break through the barrier and destroy us all."

Rianna nodded. "We'll stop them..." She trailed off at a strange whirring sound. "What's that?"

"I don't know." Aislinn frowned. "I've never heard anything like it."

The sound grew louder, and a dark shape appeared in the sky. It was huge, and it reminded Rianna of a giant flying saucer from a science fiction movie. As it got closer, the shape took form, and she recognized it was a dragon. Something...someone...rode on its back.

"Run," said Abby a second before the dragon let loose a blast of dragonfire.

Rianna screamed and grabbed Lirra, running away from the flames. Heat flared near her back, and she knew they wouldn't be fast enough to escape.

Lirra shoved her to the ground and threw herself over her, shielding Rianna with her body. "Stay down."

"No, Lirra." Rianna tried to push her off, but the orc warrior was too heavy.

"Stop it, Rianna. I'm trying to protect you and the babe." Lirra grunted as the dragonfire hit her, and she cried out in pain.

"Lirra?" Rianna struggled frantically to free herself, but the orc was practically inert and unmovable.

The dragonfire stopped, and Lirra slumped fully to the ground, bearing down on her. Rianna finally managed to wiggle out from under her sister-in-law, only to see the orc's green skin was charred and burned. Her eyes were closed, and she wasn't moving.

"No..." Rianna crawled over to her, tears streaming down her face. "No, no, no." She cradled Lirra's head in her lap, gently stroking her hair. "Please, Lirra. Please don't die." She let out a little sob of relief when the orc's chest rose and fell. "Keep breathing."

Noise and chaos surrounded her, and she looked up, realizing most of the witches had fled or were disappearing. She didn't know that spell and refused to abandon Lirra anyway, so she braced herself as the dragon approached.

The black dragon landed, and the rider dismounted. It was a man, and he was tall and muscular, with dark blond hair and golden eyes. He wore black armor that fit him like a glove, and he carried a sword and a shield. He was handsome but sent a chill down her spine.

"Who are you?" asked Rianna as fiercely as she could manage.

"I'm Theron, and I'm here to claim mates." He looked her over. "You'll do."

"I'm not your mate."

"You will be, human. You and any others I take."

"I'm already mated to an orc."

"I don't care." He smirked. "I'm a kattarin. I can make you my mate if I choose to."

Rianna glared at him. "I'm pregnant."

Theron's eyes narrowed. "I can fix that." Without warning, he lifted his hand and fired a bolt of magic at her.

She screamed and ducked, but it was too late. The magic hit

her, followed by searing pain in her abdomen. She clutched her stomach and curled up on the ground, crying out in agony. The connection she felt with her baby suddenly felt tenuous, and she closed her eyes, funneling all her magic into countering his attempts to force her to miscarry.

"You're not going to win, human. You're weak, and I'm powerful."

She ignored him, focusing on her unborn child. She felt the link strengthen again and breathed a sigh of relief. "You're not going to kill my baby."

"We'll see about that." He raised his hand again, but before he could fire another bolt of magic, he was knocked aside by a massive black wolf.

The wolf attacked him, biting and clawing at him as he fought back. The two of them were locked in a fierce battle, and it was clear the wolf was no match for the kattarin.

Rianna watched in horror as the wolf was thrown across the clearing, crashing into a tree. The wolf let out a howl of pain and shifted back into its human form. The elderly black man was unfamiliar to her but clearly a Mythic.

In seconds, more wolves appeared, surrounding the area, and edging warily around Theron's dragon.

"*Undo its harness,*" shouted a voice in her mind.

She winced but focused on the golden bridle in the dragon's mouth. She winced in horror when she realized someone— unquestionably Theron—had drilled it into the poor thing's flesh. It surely felt every tug and must be in constant agony.

"I'm sorry," she whispered as she used her magic to undo the bolts in its flesh. "You poor thing."

The dragon shook itself free of the harness and took flight, circling above the clearing. It let out a roar of rage and dove at Theron, knocking him to the ground.

The wolves swarmed over him, and Rianna watched as the dragon joined the fray. The fight was brutal, with the dragons and wolves tearing into Theron before a bright blast of light, like looking straight into a solar eclipse, filled the clearing. Wind blew around them, and the Mythics fighting him were tossed aside.

Theron got to his feet, looking battered but nowhere near defeated. He sneered at her. "There are plenty of Omegas to help add to my kind. You're not even that pretty." He launched himself into the air, shifting into a massive gold cat creature with wings.

She sat up slowly, testing the connection with her baby first thing. It felt strong, and his or her presence was easy to discern. She was confident Theron hadn't forced her to miscarry.

The dragon, in the meantime, had flown after him, and the two of them were engaged in a vicious aerial battle.

"Rianna."

She turned to see Halox kneeling beside her, his eyes full of concern. "Halox."

"Are you hurt?"

"No, but Lirra is." She gestured to the orc. "She saved my life."

"I'll get her to the healers." Halox picked up his sister and carried her away.

Rianna turned back to the battle, watching with wide eyes as the dragon and the kattarin fought.

The dragon seemed to be winning, but it was injured and tiring quickly. She could see blood dripping from its wounds, and it was struggling to stay aloft.

"No," she whispered.

The dragon let out a roar of anger and flew at Theron, slamming into him, but it sent the dragon spiraling to the ground. The impact was hard enough to shake the earth around them, and she stumbled as she rushed to the fallen dragon.

The beast was badly hurt, its black scales covered in blood. It was gasping for breath, and one of its wings was broken.

Acting on instinct from having observed the orc healers while recalling a spell from the grimoire, she cast a healing spell.

The dragon's injuries began to close, and its breathing eased. It looked at her with gratitude in its eyes. "Thank you, human."

"You're welcome." She reached out and touched its snout. "Rest now. You need to heal." When she looked up into the sky, Theron was gone.

CHAPTER THIRTEEN—HALOX

He had an uneasy feeling the moment she left, and it persisted throughout the next hour. Halox tried to tell himself it was simply not having her near him, but he couldn't escape the feeling of impending doom. He was discussing it with Halox and Caius when Aislinn suddenly appeared in their midst.

"I'm sorry to interrupt, but we're under attack. Theron has returned."

Halox's blood ran cold, recognizing the name. Theron was the stuff of legends, even though the orcs hadn't deal with him or other kattarin in a thousand years. "Where's Rianna?"

"She and Lirra were with my coven when he arrived. We were discussing the nemataurs when the dragon attacked. We barely escaped with our lives."

His heart clenched. "Where is my mate?"

"She stayed behind to try to save Lirra. I'm sorry." She looked genuinely remorseful. "I couldn't get past the dragon, so I came to you."

He grasped her arm, aware she could probably disappear in

a flash. "Show me where."

"Of course." She gently pulled away. "We were meeting in the Wolven territory. Our coven has formed an alliance with them since my great-grandmother discovered she's the fated mate of their Elder."

Halox nodded. "I know of them. We have no quarrel."

"Good. Then you can come with me."

"I'm coming too," said Caius.

"As am I." Taxlos' expression was grim.

"Very well." Aislinn waved her hands, and a portal opened. "Follow me."

She led them through the portal, and they emerged in the middle of a forest. There were wolves everywhere, and a large black one was leaning against a tree, bleeding heavily. An elderly woman sat beside him, and the Wolven in his human form was quite old too. He must be the Elder.

"Where is Rianna?" demanded Halox.

"She's over there." Aislinn pointed to a small group of people gathered nearby.

Halox hurried over to them, pushing his way through the crowd until he saw Rianna cradling his sister's head in her lap. "Rianna.

She looked up, and he could see the fear and pain in her eyes. "Halox."

"Are you hurt?"

"No, but Lirra is." She gestured to the orc. "She saved my life."

He knelt beside her, examining Lirra. She was unconscious, but her pulse was steady. "She's alive."

Rianna nodded. "She protected me."

"I'll get her to the healers." Halox picked up his sister and carried her away, hating to be parted from his mate, but his sister needed him more for the moment. When he'd handed her off to the healers, he turned and saw his mate with a dragon in front of her.

With a feral cry, he rushed forward to protect her, but she held up a hand. "It's okay, Halox. He's a friend."

The dragon looked at him with amusement. "I'm not going to hurt her, orc. I'm grateful for her assistance."

"Assistance?" He looked at Rianna. "What happened?"

She told him about the battle, and he listened in shock. "You faced a kattarin alone and survived?"

"Not alone. The wolves helped me." She gestured to the large, black wolf. "He saved my life by attacking Theron and telling me to unharness the dragon. At least, I think he was the one who told me that."

The elderly man rose, shifting to his wolf form before reappearing, healed, in his human form. "Yes, that was me. I'm Darius, the alpha of the Wolven pack."

"I'm Halox. Thank you for protecting my mate."

Darius shrugged. "My mate is part of the coven Theron attacked."

"I thank you," said the dragon as he shifted into a handsome male form.

Halox scowled at him. "You're naked."

The dragon laughed. "So is Darius, but you don't protest that." He winked at Rianna, which irritated Halox all the more.

Halox growled. "You're a dragon, and you're naked."

"I'm a shifter, and my name is Nykos." He grinned at Rianna. "And I owe you a debt of gratitude, little witch. I would have died if you hadn't healed me."

Rianna blushed. "I was just returning the favor. You saved us."

Halox planted himself firmly between them, not liking the openly flirtatious smile on the dragon-man's face. "You can repay your debt by finding some clothes."

Nykos chuckled. "I suppose I should." He looked at Rianna. "I'll return shortly."

"I'll be here."

Halox growled again, and Nykos laughed as he walked

away.

Rianna poked him in the side. "Stop growling, Halox. He's a friend."

"He was naked and flirting with you."

"Was he? I never noticed." She put her arms around him. "How is Lirra?"

"Fine," said his sister gruffly from behind them before he could answer. When they turned, she was visibly burned, but the wounds were rapidly fading. "I'm fine, Rianna. Thanks for staying with me, but you should have run."

"I couldn't leave you."

Lirra smiled. "You're a good female. I'm glad you're my brother's mate."

"Me too." Rianna hugged Halox. "I missed him."

"I missed you too, love." He looked around. "What are we up against?"

To his surprise, the coven of witches appeared, seeming to pop right into existence. "It's a lot," said Aislinn, sounding tired.

"I'll send for refreshments," said Darius. "I'm sure we're all hungry and thirsty."

"Thank you," said Aislinn.

While they waited for the refreshments, Rianna introduced the witches to Halox, Taxlos, and Caius.

Taxlos bowed to Aislinn. "I'm pleased to meet you, Keeper."

"You're an Alpha, aren't you?" she asked.

"I am."

"You're seeking your mate."

He nodded, looking surprised. "I am. Her name is Erin, and she slipped away." He grunted. "Why am I telling you this?"

"Magic," said Aislinn with a small smile. "People often confide in me without prompting. It's either a gift or curse, depending on the situation."

"I see." Taxlos studied her. "You're not afraid of me."

"Should I be?"

"Most humans are."

"I'm not most humans."

"Clearly."

Aislinn smiled. "I sense you're a good male, Taxlos." She looked at Rianna. "It's true my coven held a more rigid view about Mythics, based on historical accountings, but our opinions are changing one Mythic at a time. My great-grandmother is mated to the Alpha of the Wolven pack, though they probably won't have offspring at this age." She smiled in the direction of the elderly couple before looking at Rianna again. "And my friend here has found a good mate as well."

"I'm glad you approve," said Halox dryly.

"I do, and I apologize for my earlier behavior. I was wrong."

"I accept your apology, Keeper."

She nodded. "Now that's out of the way, we need to discuss what's happening, and the best way to convince the Mythics and humans an alliance is the only way to defeat Theron and the nemataurs."

A few minutes later, they were all seated around a table, eating and drinking while Aislinn explained what had transpired. Halox was horrified to learn of the nemataurs, and he shuddered to think of his mate being taken by a kattarin.

"He said I'd do as one of his mates and said he'd make me his." Her voice trembled. "He hurt our baby."

"What?" He put his hand on her stomach. "How?"

"He tried to force me to miscarry, but I managed to stop him. I don't know how, but I did."

"You're a witch." Aislinn's tone was matter-of-fact. "You're a powerful one, and you're carrying a half-orc baby. You're also a healer, and you have a connection to the child. You're more powerful than you realize, Rianna."

"I didn't know that." She looked troubled. "I don't want to

be powerful if it means putting my child in danger."

"Your child will be powerful too. I can already feel her..." She trailed off, clearing her throat. "I'm sorry. I shouldn't have told you that."

She looked at Aislinn in surprise. "It's a girl?"

Halox grinned. "It's a girl?" he echoed.

"I think so." Aislinn smiled. "I can usually tell."

He leaned over and kissed Rianna. "A daughter."

"Yes." She was smiling, but her eyes were troubled. "I'm worried about her."

"Why?"

"What if Theron succeeds in bringing the nemataurs through the portal?"

"He won't." Halox was determined to protect his mate and their daughter, along with the others living on Earth. "We'll stop him."

"How?" asked Rianna.

"I don't know yet, but we will." He wrapped his arms around her. "We will."

They finished their meal and discussed strategy, deciding the best way to approach both the humans and the other Mythics. As they talked, his attention was on the plan, but he didn't release Rianna at all. He couldn't let her out of his sight or any farther away than the length of his arm.

When the talks concluded, Aislinn opened them a mini portal to save time and energy traveling back to Fort Tyron, since Lirra was still healing, and Rianna looked exhausted. Once he had her back in the tent, he told himself to let her rest, but he couldn't stop touching her.

"What's wrong, Halox?"

"Nothing." He nuzzled her neck. "I can't get enough of you."

"I know the feeling." She stroked his hair. "I love you, Halox."

"I love you too, Rianna." He kissed her slowly, savoring the taste and feel of her. "I want to make love to you, but I don't want to hurt you or the baby."

"You won't hurt us. I promise." She smiled. "Make love to me. I need you."

He groaned and kissed her again, his lips moving over hers in a slow, sensual kiss. He licked and nibbled her lower lip, teasing her until she moaned and parted her lips. He slid his tongue inside, stroking and exploring her mouth. She tasted sweet, like honey and berries, and he couldn't get enough.

He deepened the kiss, his tongue tangling with hers as he explored her mouth. She responded eagerly, her tongue dancing with his as she pressed her body against his. Her hands roamed over his back and shoulders, and he could scent her arousal.

He broke the kiss and looked down at her, admiring the flush on her cheeks and the way her pupils were dilated with desire. "I want to take you like this, with you on your back so I can see your face."

"Yes." She tugged at his armor. "Take it off."

He complied, stripping off his clothing before helping her remove hers. He took his time, kissing and caressing every inch of her skin as he revealed it. She was beautiful, her brown skin smooth and soft under his fingers.

He cupped her breasts, stroking her nipples with his thumbs. She moaned and arched her back, pressing her breasts into his hands. "That feels good."

"It does." He bent his head and took one nipple into his mouth, sucking and licking it until it was hard and pebbled. He moved to the other one, lavishing the same attention on it.

She writhed under him, her hips bucking as she sought friction. "Halox, please."

He smiled and kissed his way down her body, pausing to lick and suck on her belly button as he made his way to her pussy. He parted her folds with his fingers, exposing her clit, which he flicked with his tongue, and she cried out, her hips jerking.

He continued to tease her, licking and sucking her clit until she was on the verge of orgasm. Just before she could go over the edge, he stopped, pulling back to look at her. "I want to feel you come on my cock."

"Yes." She reached for him, and he settled between her legs, lining his shaft up with her dripping entrance.

He thrust into her in one smooth motion, burying himself in her tight cunt. She was so wet and hot, and he groaned as her inner muscles clenched around him. "Perfect."

"Yes." She wrapped her legs around his waist, urging him to move.

He began to thrust, his pace slow and steady as he worked his way in and out of her. He wanted to savor this moment, to draw it out as long as possible, and to make it last forever.

She met his every stroke, her body moving with his as they found their rhythm. They moved together, their bodies in perfect sync as they made love. His chest ached with emotion, and he knew he would never love anyone as much as he loved Rianna. She was his everything, and he would do whatever it took to keep her safe.

The pleasure built, and he increased his pace, his movements becoming more urgent as he neared his climax. She clung to him, her nails digging into his back as she urged him on. "Harder, my love. Make me yours."

He growled and slammed into her, his thrusts growing harder and faster as he chased his release. She cried out, her body tensing as she came, her inner walls squeezing his cock. The sensation was too much, and he followed her over the edge, his orgasm washing over him in waves of pure bliss. He emptied himself into her, filling her with his cum as he claimed her once more.

They stayed like that for a long moment, basking in the afterglow of their lovemaking. He finally withdrew and rolled to his side, gathering her into his arms. "I never want to let you go."

"I don't want you to." She rested her head on his chest.

They laid in silence, and he listened to her breathing even out as she drifted off to sleep. As he held her, he vowed to do everything in his power to protect her and their child. Nothing would ever harm them as long as he was alive.

CHAPTER FOURTEEN—RIANNA

She stood beside Halox almost a month later as the Keeper coven stood with them. Aislinn was addressing the human delegates who'd gathered for another summit, this time with much tighter security, including Wolven guards prowling the perimeter in their animal forms.

"We've come together to address a new threat to Earth. It's not the Mythics, and it's not the humans. It's a group of creatures called nemataurs, and they're ancient and evil. They want to destroy all life on Earth."

"Why should we believe you?" asked Mayor Monarky. "Why should we trust you?"

"Because we're not asking for anything in return. We're not here to negotiate a treaty or demand anything from you. We're here to warn you, because if we don't work together, we're all going to die," said Aislinn.

"If these nemataurs are so dangerous, why haven't they come through the portal yet?" asked the mayor.

"They're working with a Mythic named Theron, and he's

been trying to break through the barrier. Their kind hasn't been able to cross the portal in the past because of an old and powerful spell that fueled a barrier designed to keep them out, but now that the supercollider has weakened the barrier, they might be able to do it," said Aislinn.

Monarky frowned. "What do you mean?"

"The supercollider experiment that opened the portals also created a breach in the barrier that was like a…filter over the portal. The magical barrier has been in place for centuries, and it was the only thing that kept the nemataurs from coming through in the past," said Aislinn. "Before our...the portal closed so mysteriously, the Mythics and the humans kept the barrier strong. When the portal closed, there was no reason to keep up the barrier, at least on Earth, so no one maintained the magic, but the barrier still stands to this day. It's very weak, and now that the portal is open, and the Mythics are back, the barrier needs to be reinforced."

"How do you know all this?" asked Monarky. He looked skeptical.

"I'm a witch with access to all the archives, and I'm the Keeper of the Portal."

"What's a Keeper?"

"It's a title passed down to the strongest magic user in my coven. I'm the current Keeper, and it's my responsibility to maintain the barrier and protect the portal," said Aislinn.

"Can you prove it?" asked Monarky.

"You're not going to believe it unless you see it with your own eyes, are you?" Aislinn sighed. "Very well." She waved her hand, and a shimmering circle appeared in the middle of the room.

Rianna jumped back in shock at the sight of the smudgy, black creatures pressed together, fighting and snapping at each other. "Don't let them through." Her heart leapt into her throat as she issued the warning.

"They can't come through. This is a viewing portal of the

nemataurs' home realm." As Aislinn explained, three of the monsters grabbed hold of a smaller one among them. It was difficult to tell what they were doing, but all movement stopped in the smallest one, and then they tore into it with their teeth. The creature screamed, and Rianna felt sick.

"What are they doing?" asked Monarky.

"The nemataurs feed primarily on life essence. The stronger ones prey on the weaker ones even among their own kind. They drained it and then ate the meat."

"Oh, no." Rianna felt faint. "That's horrible."

"It is, but it's how they survive. They're a parasitic species, and they'll drain the life out of everything on Earth if they get through the portal." Aislinn's expression became grimmer still.

"How do we stop them?" asked Monarky.

"The only way to stop them is to close the portal or strengthen the barrier," said Aislinn. "The magic is weak, and it's getting weaker every day, because it's dissipating from the spell...whatever kept the portal closed and is returning to humans. Most of us don't know how to use the magic, and we don't have time to learn." The witch's shoulders straightened. "We need help from the Mythics, because we can't close the portal or keep the barrier strong on our own."

"What can we do?" asked Monarky.

"You can help by keeping the peace and making sure the Mythics and humans don't kill each other while we figure out how to stop the nemataurs," said Aislinn. "Please agree to the alliance, so we can focus on a common enemy. We can't afford to be divided."

"I'll agree to the alliance on one condition," said Monarky.

"What's that?" asked Aislinn.

"The Mythics have to stay in designated areas and abide by human laws while in our realm."

"We can't agree to that," said Halox. "The Mythics have their own laws and customs, and we can't expect them to change overnight."

"Then we have nothing to discuss," said Monarky. The other humans around him nodded.

"We're not asking them to change their ways, but they can't just run wild in our cities," said Ursula Grundy, the French president. "We have to find a compromise."

"What about if they follow their own customs in their territories, and they agree to abide by human laws in human areas?" asked Rianna.

"That could work," said Monarky.

"We could also set up some sort of liaison system," said Rianna. "The Mythics could appoint someone to represent them, and the humans could do the same. That way, there's a direct line of communication between the two sides."

"I think that's a good idea," said Ursula.

"I agree," said Monarky, and the other human leaders nodded. He shot a challenging look at Halox. "What do you say, General?"

Halox nodded. "I think that's a fair compromise."

"Good. Then let's get started," said Monarky.

Rianna breathed a sigh of relief as the humans and Mythics began to talk. She was glad the alliance seemed to be forming, but the real battle was still ahead of them. The nemataurs were a formidable enemy, and they needed to be stopped before it was too late.

As the meeting went on, Rianna felt a strange, prickling sensation in the air. It was as if something was watching them, and the feeling grew stronger with each passing minute.

"Do you feel that?" she whispered to Aislinn.

The witch nodded. "Theron is here. He's spying on us."

"What should we do?" Remembering her confrontation with him, Rianna's stomach churned.

"We need to get these people out of here. It's not safe." Aislinn raised her voice. "Everyone, we need to evacuate. There's a kattarin nearby, and he's a very dangerous Mythic named Theron. Please, everyone, leave the building immediately."

The humans looked at her in confusion, but the Mythics reacted instantly. They began herding the humans toward the exits, and the Wolven guards shifted to their animal forms, growling and snapping at the air.

"What's going on?" shouted Monarky.

"The Mythic Aislinn told you about, Theron, is here. We need to get you out of here before he attacks," said Halox.

"I'm not leaving until I get an explanation," said Monarky.

"There's no time," said Aislinn. "Just get out of the building."

The mayor shook his head. "No. This could be a trap...or some power maneuver. I'm not going anywhere with them."

"Fine. Stay here and die," said Aislinn as she turned toward the others, opening a mini portal. "This will take us to the Wolven territory." She raised her voice to the humans. "I suggest you come if you like being alive, but that's your decision. I'm not waiting around for Theron to show himself."

The humans looked at each other uncertainly, but when one of them stepped forward and disappeared into the portal, the rest followed suit, including Monarky.

Once they were gone, Aislinn looked at Halox. "Do your people want to stay or go?"

"We're not cowards," said Halox. "We'll fight." As he spoke, the orcs gathered around him in a defensive formation. The Wolven guards joined them, and the centaurs fell in with the group. He looked at Rianna. "Get her out of here please, Keeper."

"No, I'm not leaving you." She clutched Halox's arm. "I won't."

"Rianna, it's not safe for you here." Halox's tone was gentle but firm. "I need to know you and our child are secure."

"I'm not leaving." She clung to him, refusing to let go.

"Rianna..."

"Halox, please." She looked up at him, tears in her eyes.

"I'm scared, but I'm more scared of losing you. I can't leave you."

"All right." He pulled her into his arms. "You can stay, but you have to promise me you'll stay behind me and out of the way."

"I will." She buried her face in his chest, inhaling his familiar scent. "I love you, Halox."

"I love you too." He kissed her forehead. "If we're losing, promise me you'll leave with Aislinn. If you don't promise, I'll carry you through that portal myself now and deal with your rage later. Promise me."

She nodded reluctantly. "I promise."

"Good." He released her and turned to the others. "Let's get ready for battle."

The Mythics and witches prepared themselves, and the tension in the air made the hairs on her neck stand up. Rianna stayed with Aislinn, who was murmuring spells under her breath.

"What are you doing?" she asked.

"I'm preparing a shield for us. I'm also reinforcing the travel portal to keep it open in case we need a hasty escape." She tipped her head slightly in its direction. "Help me cast strengthening spells for the warriors."

Rianna bit her lip as she searched her memory for the invocation. "I remember the spell, but I've never done it before."

"You can do it. I'll guide you." Without hesitation, Aislinn grasped her hands, and Rianna felt the surge of magic flowing between them. "Now, repeat after me."

They repeated the chant, and with the magic flowing between them, it strengthened the warriors. It was an exhilarating feeling, and she understood why Aislinn had chosen this path. Magic was intoxicating, and the more she used it, the more she craved it.

"Enough." Aislinn pulled away. "You'll burn out."

"I'm fine." She was a little dizzy, but the rush of magic was addictive.

"You're not. You're pregnant, and you're not used to using this much magic."

"I can handle it."

"You can't." Aislinn's tone was sharp. "I'm sorry, but you can't. You're not trained, and you're carrying a baby. You'll hurt yourself, and you'll hurt your child." Her tone gentled. "Magic is incredible but can be addictive. You need to get used to using it and adapt, or you might be consumed by it."

"I see." Rianna was suddenly aware of the weight of her unborn child, and she placed her hand on her belly protectively. "I'm sorry. I didn't realize." Guilt washed over her for putting her child at risk.

"It's okay. Just be careful. Magic is a powerful tool, but it can also be dangerous." Aislinn gave her an encouraging smile. "You did well though. You're a natural."

"Thank you." She looked around the room. "What do we do now?"

"We wait for Theron to make his move." Aislinn glanced at the ceiling. "He's up there somewhere, watching us."

"Can you sense him?"

"Yes, but he's cloaking himself somehow. I can't pinpoint his location."

"I can." Rianna closed her eyes, reaching out with her senses. She could feel the kattarin's presence, and it was strong and malevolent. "How can I sense him so acutely?"

"Likely because he attacked you, and you pushed back. That kind of encounter can leave an extra awareness...almost like a stain or a scar on your very magical essence. He can't hide from you as easily as he can the rest of us."

"I see." She opened her eyes, focusing on the area where she sensed the kattarin. "He's up there." She pointed to the ceiling. As if on cue, the roof exploded inward, and the kattarin landed in the middle of the room.

The Mythics and humans rushed forward to attack, but the kattarin roared and unleashed a blast of energy that knocked them all backward. Rianna watched in horror as the Mythics and witches struggled to rise, their movements sluggish and uncoordinated. Whatever the kattarin had done to them, it had sapped their strength.

Fear clawed at her insides, and she dared risk performing a strengthening spell, focusing its benefit solely on Halox. He had to survive. She refused to live without him.

CHAPTER FIFTEEN—HALOX

Theron's blast of power left him disoriented, but he struggled to his feet, his body heavy and his mind foggy. He could see the other Mythics and humans struggling to stand, and they were in trouble.

"I'm here for the witch." Theron's voice was like nails on a chalkboard, and Halox winced as he tried to focus on the kattarin. "Give her to me, and I'll leave."

"Never." Halox forced himself to his feet, his body protesting the movement. "You're not taking my mate."

"The other witch," said Theron with clear impatience. "She's an ideal Omega for my offspring and as yet unclaimed. I want her."

"She's not yours," said Halox, his voice hoarse as he fought against the effects of the kattarin's power. "She has no mate."

"I'm her mate." Theron's voice was filled with conviction. "I'm the only one worthy of her, and I'll destroy anyone who stands in my way."

"You'll have to go through me first." The threat felt a little empty, since he was so weak, but he straightened his posture and took a steady step forward. When he dared glance at Rianna, she was staring at him and whispering something, her lips moving.

In a second, everything shifted. The weakness disappeared as a surge of energy coursed through his veins. He felt stronger than he ever had, and he knew she'd given him a boost. He met her gaze and nodded, hoping she'd understand his silent message.

He turned back to Theron. "You're not taking her or any of the witches. Leave now, and I'll spare your life."

"You're in no position to make threats, orc." Theron snorted. "You're barely standing."

"I'm not alone." Halox gestured to the Mythics and witches slowly rising to their feet. "We're not giving up."

"You're fools. All of you." Theron's tone was dismissive. "You're wasting your time and energy fighting me when you should be focused on the real threat. The nemataurs are coming, and they'll destroy you all."

"Not if we stop you," said Halox.

"You can't stop me. No one can." Theron's eyes narrowed. "But I can give you a reprieve. I'll take the witches and leave, and you can enjoy your pathetic lives for a few more months."

"We'll never surrender to you," said Halox.

"You'll die then," said Theron dismissively.

"We'll never surrender," said Halox.

"So be it." Theron lunged forward, his talons outstretched as he shifted into his winged-cat form and aimed for Halox's throat. Halox dodged the blow, swinging his axe at Theron's neck. The blade connected, and he heard the satisfying sound of metal slicing through flesh.

Theron roared in pain and anger, whirling around to face Halox. "You'll pay for that, orc."

"I doubt it." Halox swung his axe again, this time aiming for the kattarin's head. Theron ducked, narrowly avoiding the blade. He launched himself at Halox, knocking him to the ground.

He grunted as the kattarin's weight bore down on him, but he managed to keep a grip on his axe. He brought it up, burying the blade in the kattarin's shoulder.

Theron howled in pain, rearing back and momentarily releasing his hold. He took advantage of the opportunity, rolling to his feet and swinging his axe again. He caught Theron in the side, and the kattarin staggered backward, blood pouring from the wound.

"This isn't over, orc." Theron's words were laced with venom. "I'll take what's mine."

"I don't think so." Aislinn's voice rang out, and Halox saw her hurl a bolt of energy at the kattarin. It hit Theron in the chest, sending him flying backward. He crashed into the wall with a loud thud, his body crumpling to the floor.

"Is he dead?" asked Halox.

"I don't know." Aislinn approached the fallen kattarin cautiously, her hands outstretched. "I can't tell."

"Be careful." Halox moved to her side, his axe at the ready.

Aislinn knelt beside Theron, her hand hovering over his body. Suddenly, the kattarin sprang to life, lunging at her with his claws extended. He knocked her to the ground, his talons digging into her throat as he pinned her down.

"You'll be my mate, witch." Theron's voice was low and menacing. "You'll bear my children and serve me."

"Never." Aislinn spat in his face, her eyes blazing with defiance as Halox charged forward, his axe raised, looking for an opening.

Theron dragged his muzzle against Aislinn's throat to scent-mark her, and she shouted in outrage. "Get off me."

"I'll claim you now and breed you while your pitiful allies watch. Then you'll be mine."

"I'll never be yours." Aislinn's voice was strong and filled with conviction. "I'll kill myself before I let you touch me."

"You won't." Theron laughed, the sound sending shivers down Halox's spine.

Deciding he had to risk it, he brought up the axe, hoping to strike Theron's spine. The axe sliced through the air before stopping abruptly. He frowned in confusion until a flickering form solidified. Instinctively, he bared his teeth at the vampire. "Back away from your master, or I'll take your head too."

The vampire's green eyes flared red. "He's not my master, and you could kill my mate. Your axe is too close to Aislinn."

Halox exhaled slowly, pulling back his axe when the vampire released it. "Who are you?"

"I'm Lucian D'Arcy, and the call of my mate woke me from my slumber." He looked at Aislinn, eyes burning with hunger. "For her, I'll walk in the sunlight."

"You're a vampire." He was surprised. "I thought you couldn't do that."

"I'm old enough that the sun no longer affects me." His attention shifted to Theron. "Release my mate, kattarin."

"She's my mate. I claimed her because of her magic. She'll make a fine Omega—the first of many." He lewdly thrust against her. "Watch me defile her, bloodsucker."

"No." The word came out as a growl as Lucian surged forward, his fangs bared as he grabbed the kattarin by the back of his neck. He yanked him off Aislinn, throwing him across the room as if he weighed nothing.

Theron slammed into the wall, his body crumpling to the floor. He laid still for a moment before his eyes snapped open, and he shifted into his human form, his face contorted with rage.

"I'll kill you for that, vampire."

"You can try." Lucian's tone was bored as he stalked toward the kattarin. "But you'll fail."

"We'll see about that." Theron snarled, launching himself at Lucian. He shifted into his winged-cat form, his talons and teeth flashing as he attacked.

Lucian met him head on, his own fangs and claws out as he defended his mate. The two creatures clashed, their bodies colliding in a flurry of flesh and fur.

Halox moved to Aislinn's side, helping her to her feet. "Are you all right?"

"I'm fine." She brushed herself off, her eyes fixed on the battle raging before them. "We need to help him."

He nodded, his gaze settling on Rianna first, to assure himself she was still uninjured. She was whispering another spell, and he nodded to Aislinn. "Should she be doing so much magic?"

"No, but she's stubborn, and she loves you." She smiled. "Her magic is strong, and she's determined to protect you."

"I know." He moved closer to Rianna, wanting to shield her from the violence, but it reached him before he cold. Lucian and Theron rolled into him, knowing him off his feet and into the fray. Taxlos let out a howl of anger, and soon, orcs surrounded the pile. Halox did his best to determine against whom he was striking, but it was a muddled, bloody mess.

When he finally found his way to his feet, he froze as Rianna and Aislinn, hands bound, shouted a spell. In seconds, everything slowed. The combatants floated away from the huddle on the floor until Theron was visible again. Lucian was drinking his blood, but the kattarin was about to disembowel him in his distraction. With time temporarily slowed, Halox swung his axe in his hand over his shoulder. With a fierce grunt, he drove it into the kattarin's back, severing his spine.

Time resumed its normal course, and Theron slumped forward onto Lucian, who finished draining the kattarin and tossed aside the body. He stood, his eyes glowing with satisfaction as he looked at Aislinn.

"Mate."

Aislinn nodded, her expression wary. "I'm yours."

"And I am yours." He held out his hand to her. "Come to me."

"I will." She took a hesitant step toward him, her eyes locked on his. "Soon. I need to finish here. We need to ensure the humans are safe, and the nemataurs are contained."

"They are for now." He shrugged. "They can't cross the barrier, and they're not as strong as they once were. They've been feeding off each other for centuries, and their numbers are dwindling. Without someone on this side trying to bring them through, I don't see how they'll succeed."

"How do you know that?" asked Halox, suspicious of the vampire.

"My power comes with a gift for Seeing whatever I'd like to know. It's imprecise, but I'm confident the nemataurs are currently trapped in their realm." Lucian looked wary. "I'm old enough to remember when the portal was still open between the realms, and I helped with the magical reinforcement of the barrier." He gave Aislinn a small smile. "I suspect that spell is how your foremothers got the idea of closing the portal entirely."

Halox laughed as Aislinn flinched.

"You know about that?" she asked the vampire.

Rianna came to stand beside Halox, putting her arm around his waist as they watched the two prospective mates.

"I do, and I don't blame you for it. The Mythics weren't always the most civilized of creatures. We needed a reset." He looked at Aislinn. "Now that I've found you, I think we're ready to come together again."

"What do you mean?" asked Halox.

"I mean that I think it's time for the Mythics and humans to live in peace, and to maybe even coexist," said Lucian.

"That's a big change," said Halox.

"It is, but it's also a necessary one," said Lucian. "You must convince the humans to agree...and for that to work, I suggest you not yet reveal that the nemataurs can't cross into this realm without a champion on this side."

"Why?" asked Aislinn.

"Because if they think the threat is still imminent, they're more likely to cooperate," said Rianna.

"Exactly," said Lucian. "If you want the humans to accept the Mythics, you have to give them a common enemy—one that's a true threat, if not so urgently now."

"You're suggesting we lie?" asked Halox.

"No, I'm suggesting you alter certain truths," said Lucian. "It's not lying. It's politics."

"I don't know..." Aislinn hesitated.

"It's not a bad idea," said Halox. "At least not at first. Once the Mythics have proven themselves to the humans, we can tell them the truth."

"I suppose we could do that," said Aislinn doubtfully.

"I'm sure the humans will agree to the alliance," said Rianna. "They have to see that we're better together than apart, especially if the nemataurs are a threat."

"They are a threat," said Aislinn. "They're a very real threat, and we need to stop them from crossing through the portal."

"Then we need to work together," said Halox.

"We do," said Aislinn.

"We also need to hide certain aspects to get the humans to agree." Rianna sent Halox a small smile. "Trust me when I say, I know how determined we can be when we decide on a course. Aislinn tried to warn me what would happen if I created the black hole with the supecollider, and I ignored her."

"That's true." Halox nodded. "Humans can be very stubborn."

"So can Mythics," said Aislinn, her tone dry. "You're just as bad as we are."

"Maybe," said Halox, "But we can work together to solve this problem. That's the important thing."

"It is." Aislinn sighed. "I guess we can do it your way, but we have to be honest with the humans eventually."

"There is definitely still a threat," said Lucian in a soothing tone. "If anyone was working with Theron, they could still be scheming to bring over the nemataurs. Don't let your conscious twinge too much, my mate. The humans need to be protected, and we need to be able to do that."

"All right." Aislinn nodded. "We'll do it your way."

"Good." Halox smiled. "Now, let's go talk to the humans and get this alliance signed."

CHAPTER SIXTEEN—RIANA

Aislinn's mini portal had held, so the group stepped through, soon finding themselves in the clearing in the middle of the Midwood, in Prospect Park. It was the same place she'd faced off with Theron, when Darius and the Wolven had appeared at the witches' behest.

The mayor was there, along with the other human leaders. They looked shocked to see the Mythics, but they quickly recovered.

"What happened?" asked Monarky. "Where's the kattarin?"

"He's dead," said Halox. "We killed him."

"You did?" Monarky looked skeptical. "How?"

"We worked together," said Aislinn. "The Mythics and the witches."

"That's impossible," said Monarky. "There's no way you could work together."

"We did," said Aislinn. "We put aside our differences and fought the common enemy."

"The kattarin," said Monarky, his tone still doubtful.

"Yes," said Aislinn. "The kattarin."

"What about the other Mythics? The ones who attacked the city?" asked Monarky. "Are they gone too?"

"They're in the mountains, and they worked for Theron because he promised to eradicate the humans and other Mythics. They could still help the nemataurs," said Lucian with a hint of warning, stepping forward to introduce himself.

He spoke so earnestly that Rianna couldn't tell if he was being truthful or distorting the facts somewhat, as they'd agreed to do. She decided to trust him, though the idea of the trolls, ogres, and giants having aligned with Theron and the nemataurs frightened her. She hoped he was just making up something and sounding confident to sell the idea. "The Mythics and humans have to work together to defeat the nemataurs."

"You have to understand, this is all confusing. We just want our home back the way it was," said Monarky.

Ursula Grundy nodded. "That would be ideal. Couldn't we offer enticements for your Mythics to return to their worlds? Perhaps some human Omegas...willing, of course."

"We can't do that," said Rianna. "The Mythics need the humans as much as the humans need them. Mythics are stronger than humans, and they can help protect us from the nemataurs. If we're divided, we'll be destroyed."

"The portal is impossible to close now anyway," said Aislinn. "The magic has waned, and now it's returning to the magic users, but they don't know how to control it or use it."

"What does that mean?" asked Monarky.

"It means the portal will remain open, and Mythics will continue to come through," said Aislinn.

"What about the nemataurs?" asked Monarky.

"They can't get through the barrier if we focus on strengthening it," said Aislinn. "As long as the Mythics and humans work together, we can keep them out."

"What about the kattarin?" asked Monarky. "Are there

more of them?"

"There are, but they're not here yet," said Aislinn. "If you want to keep the portal open, you'll need to strengthen the barrier and keep the Mythics and humans working together."

"What if we don't?" The question came from a tall man with a thick, gray beard. Rianna didn't recognize him, but he seemed to be an official of some sort, judging by the way the others deferred to him.

"Then the nemataurs will come through and destroy everything," said Aislinn. "We won't survive without the Mythics, and they can't survive without us. They need Omega mates, and we need their strength."

"I see," said the man, his tone thoughtful. A faint but noticeable accent suggested he might be South African. "And you're saying that if we agree to this alliance, you'll help us keep out the nemataurs?"

"We will," said Halox. "We want to live in peace with the humans."

"We want the same," said the man. "I'm President Johan van Wyk of South Africa. I propose we form an alliance between our countries with the Mythics and create a united front against the nemataurs."

"I second the motion," said Ursula. "We need to work together to survive."

"I agree," said Mayor Monarky. "We need to unite against the threat."

One by one, the other human delegates, except for the one from Japan, voted to accept an alliance. Even Norway's delegate had changed her mind.

"I'm sorry," said the Japanese delegate. "I cannot vote to allow the Mythics to stay here. It's not safe."

Monarky looked disappointed, but he didn't argue. "Very well. We'll respect your decision, but I hope you'll reconsider in the future."

"Perhaps we will," said Hiroshi Sato, the Japanese delegate.

"For now, I wish you luck." He bowed before turning and walking away.

"That's settled then," said Monarky. "Let's sign the treaty."

With the agreement of the other nations, the treaty was quickly drafted and signed. The Mythics and humans pledged to work together to protect Earth from the nemataurs and to maintain an alliance of mutual benefit. They also agreed to set up liaisons to facilitate communication between the two sides and to establish designated areas where the Mythics could live and follow their customs. In exchange, the Mythics would provide resources and magical assistance where needed. They were bound by the agreement to only claim consenting Omegas as well.

Once the treaty was signed, everyone breathed a sigh of relief. The humans and Mythics began to mingle, and the tension in the air dissipated as they started to get to know each other. Rianna saw Lucian approach Aislinn. The witch looked nervous but didn't refuse to leave with the vampire claiming her as his mate.

A yawn caught Rianna by surprise, and Halox was at her side in an instant. "You need rest. You've done too much magic today."

"I'm okay." She stifled another yawn.

"You're not. You're exhausted." He scooped her up in his arms. "Let's go home." As he carried her away from the crowd, she rested her head on his shoulder, enjoying the feeling of safety and security that enveloped her.

"Will this really work?" she asked. "The alliance?"

"I think so," said Halox. "The Mythics and humans need each other, and we both want to survive."

"I hope you're right." She closed her eyes, letting the rhythm of his steps lull her to sleep. She woke sometime later as he entered Fort Tyron and carried her toward their tent. It was late, and the camp was quiet. She heard the soft murmur of voices and the crackle of fires, but otherwise, it was peaceful.

Halox laid her gently on their bed. "Sleep now, my love."

She snuggled into the blankets, feeling warm and safe—and not that tired. "I'm not sleepy."

He chuckled. "You were asleep in my arms a few minutes ago."

"I know, but I'm awake now." She sat up and reached for him. "Come here."

"I'm not sure that's a good idea."

"Why not?" She pouted. "I want you."

"You're pregnant, and you've done too much magic today." His voice was gentle, but his tone was firm. "You need rest."

"I promise I'll rest after you make me come," she said. "Please, Halox. I need you."

He groaned softly. "You're making it hard for me to resist you."

"I don't want you to resist me." She pulled him down onto the bed beside her, kissing him hungrily. "I want you to make love to me."

He kissed her back, his tongue exploring her mouth as his hands roamed over her body. She moaned as he cupped her breasts, his thumbs brushing over her nipples. She arched against him, desperate for more.

"Halox, please." She tugged at his clothes, eager to feel his skin against hers.

"Patience, my love." He undressed her slowly, teasing her with his touch. When she was naked, he kissed his way down her body, his lips and tongue caressing every inch of her. She writhed beneath him, gasping as he licked and sucked her sensitive nipples.

He continued his exploration, his mouth moving lower until he reached her pussy. "This is my cunt, Rianna." He stroked her folds, spreading them open to expose her clit. "You're wet and swollen, and I'm going to taste you."

She cried out as he lowered his head, his tongue darting out to lick her clit. He teased her mercilessly, alternating between long, slow strokes and quick, light flicks as he eased a finger inside her. She bucked against him, her body demanding more.

"Halox, please." Her voice was a breathless whisper as she begged for release.

"Not yet." He added another finger, stretching her as he fucked her with his hand and mouth. She whimpered, her body trembling as he brought her to the edge of orgasm and then denied her.

"Please, Halox. I can't take it anymore." She was desperate for release, and he finally relented, sucking her clit as he thrust his fingers deeply inside her. She screamed as she came, shuddering with pleasure as he prolonged her climax.

When she finally came down from her high, he was watching, eyes filled with desire. "You're beautiful when you come, my Omega."

"I want to make you come too." She reached for him, her hand stroking his cock. He was rock-hard, and he groaned as she touched him.

"You're insatiable, my love." Despite his words, he thrust into her palm, his body responding to her touch.

"I want you inside me." She guided him to her entrance, moaning as he rolled onto his back and pulled her on top of him. She refused to relinquish his shaft as he positioned her how he wanted her.

"Ride me, my Omega." He gripped her hips, guiding her as she sank down on his cock. "Take your pleasure from me."

She obeyed, rocking her hips as she rode him. He filled her perfectly, and she gasped as he stretched her inner walls. He was so big, and she felt so full. It was incredible.

"That's it, my love. Take what you need." He urged her on, his hands on her hips as she moved. He was so strong and powerful, and his cock fit so perfectly inside her. She was already close to coming again, and he was holding back, waiting for her to reach her peak.

"Halox, I'm close." Her voice was a breathless whisper as she rocked her hips faster, chasing her release.

"Come for me, my Omega." He thrust up into her, his cock hitting her g-spot. She cried out as she came, her body shuddering with the force of her orgasm.

"That's it, my love." Halox held her tightly, his hips still thrusting as he sought his own release. She was still tingling from her orgasm when he came, filling her with his seed.

She collapsed against him, spent and satisfied. He wrapped his arms around her, cradling her against his chest. "Rest now, my love."

"I can't wait until you can knot me again," she said in a sleepy whisper. "I want to have those crazy, frantic days where I couldn't stand to have your cock out of me."

He chuckled. "With desires like that, you'll be constantly pregnant, my mate. We can still be close to each other and fuck like that without you needing estrus."

"I know, but I do miss your knot, and how it made me come over and over again." She yelped when he suddenly flipped her over onto her back, his fingers going between her pussy lips again. "What are you doing?"

He gave her a slow, wicked smile. "Making you come over and over again, my love."

"But I thought...oh!" She gasped as his thumb found her clit and rubbed it in tight circles. "Halox..."

"Relax, Rianna. I'll give you what you need." He kissed her, his tongue tangling with hers as his fingers brought her to the brink of another orgasm. She clung to him, her body shaking with pleasure as he pushed her over the edge.

"Halox, oh..." She shuddered as he kept rubbing her, prolonging her climax until she was a quivering mess.

"That's it, my love. Let go." He kissed her again, his lips soft and warm against hers. She melted into him, giving herself over to the sensations coursing through her body. "Good girl. Now, I'm going to fuck you again."

"Halox..." She wasn't sure she could take any more, but her body was already responding to his touch. He slid his cock into her, his movements slow and deliberate, thrusting in and out of her until she'd come over and over, as promised.

When he finally came, he buried himself deeply inside her, his body shuddering with the force of his release. "I love you, my Omega."

"I love you too, my Alpha." She snuggled against him, her heart full of joy and contentment. She was exactly where she was supposed to be, and she couldn't imagine her life without Halox by her side.

Epilogue—Rianna

Rianna clutched Halox's hand as another contraction felt like it was ripping her in half. "Never again. Do you hear me?"

"You don't mean that." Halox's voice was calm and soothing. "You're having a baby. Our baby."

"I know, but it hurts." She gritted her teeth as another wave of pain washed over her. "I hate you for doing this to me."

"You don't mean that either." He brushed a strand of hair away from her face. "You're the most amazing woman I've ever met, and you're about to bring our child into the world."

"That takes more strength than any orc warrior," said Lirra confidently, though she'd never given birth.

Rianna normally appreciated her support, but right now, she just wanted to forget about everything. "Everyone, out." Even as she barked the words, she clung to her mate's hand.

The healer also remained, but the others who'd passed the time with her, as was orc custom, dissipated without complaint.

"I'm here, Rianna." Halox's voice was a low rumble in her

ear. "I'm right here."

"I'm so glad you're here." She turned her head to look at him, her eyes filled with tears. "I'm scared."

"Don't be." He brushed a kiss against her forehead. "You're strong and brave, and you can do this."

"I'm not so sure." She winced as another contraction hit, the pain almost unbearable. "I think something's wrong."

"It's not," said the healer calmly. "Your baby is fine, and so are you. You're in labor, and that's normal. The infant is just larger than a human would be, but your Omega body knows what to do."

"Nothing about this feels normal." Rianna's voice was a hoarse whisper as she struggled to breathe through the pain.

"I know, my love." Halox's voice was a low rumble in her ear. "Just remember to breathe."

Rianna took a deep breath, trying to relax. She focused on Halox's voice, letting it anchor her as she prepared for the next contraction.

"That's it," said Halox. "You're doing great, Rianna."

"You're almost there," said the healer. "It's time to push."

Rianna bore down, pushing with all her might. The pain was excruciating, but her determination to bring her child into the world gave her the strength to endure it.

"That's it," said Halox. "You can do this, my love."

"You're almost there," said the healer. "One more big push, and the baby will be here."

Rianna took a deep breath and pushed with all her might. There was a moment of intense pressure, and then the pain subsided as the healer placed a squirming, crying infant in her arms.

"It's a girl," said the healer, smiling at Rianna and Halox. "Congratulations."

"She's perfect," said Halox, his voice thick with emotion.

"She is," said Rianna, gazing at her daughter in awe. She was a harmonious blend of human and orc—a true hybrid with her father's green skin and her mother's human features. She was sturdy and broad, with a hint of muscles already, and when she opened her eyes, they were lilac like Halox's. Her squall of protest filled the tent.

"She has the lungs of a warrior," said Halox, looking completely besotted.

"She does." Rianna smiled, feeling a rush of love for her daughter. "She's going to be strong and fierce, just like her father."

"And smart and kind, like her mother," said Halox. "May I hold her?"

"Of course." Rianna handed the baby to Halox, her heart swelling with happiness as she watched him cradle their daughter in his arms. "She's so beautiful."

"She is." Halox's voice was filled with wonder as he gazed at the baby.

"Do you have a name selected?" asked the healer.

"We do," said Rianna. "Nerissa. Nerissa Goodwin of the Clan Falcox."

"That's a beautiful name," said the healer. "I'll let the others know the good news."

"Thank you." Rianna smiled at the healer before turning her attention back to Halox and Nerissa.

"Welcome to the world, my little love," said Halox, his voice soft and tender as he gazed at his daughter. "I'm your papa, and I'll always protect you and keep you safe."

"And I'm your mama," said Rianna, her voice thick with emotion. "I love you so much, Nerissa."

The baby cooed, her tiny hand reaching out to grasp Rianna's finger. Her chest was tight as she looked at her family. She'd never imagined she'd find such happiness with an orc, but she wouldn't trade this moment for anything.

"I love you, Halox," she said, leaning in to kiss him.

"And I love you, my mate," said Halox, returning the kiss. "You've given me everything I've ever dreamed of, and more."

His eyes shone with pride as he looked at their daughter. "I'm the luckiest orc in the world."

"I'm the luckiest human," said Rianna, her eyes filling with tears. "I never imagined a black hole could lead to all this. I'm so glad it did."

"So am I." Halox's voice was husky with emotion. "So am I."

ABOUT AURELIA

Aurelia Skye is the pen name *USA Today* bestselling author Kit Tunstall uses when writing science fiction and paranormal romance, along with paranormal women's fiction. It's simply a way to separate the myriad types of stories she writes so readers know what to expect with each "author."

If you enjoyed this story and would like to receive notifications of new releases or access bonus chapters for your favorite books, please join my Mailing List**. You'll also receive free books just for joining. If you prefer to receive notifications for just one, or a few, of my pen names, you'll have the option to select which lists to subscribe to at signup.**

Milton Keynes UK
Ingram Content Group UK Ltd.
UKHW050637250923
429338UK00018B/944